The Hat Check Boy

Mike Duff

First published in 2007 by Crocus
Crocus books are published by Commonword Ltd,
6 Mount Street, Manchester M2 5NS

© Mike Duff
The right of Mike Duff to be identified as the author of this
work has been asserted by him in accordance with the
Copyright, Designs and Patents Act 1988

Crocus books are distributed by Turnaround Publisher
Services Ltd, Unit 3, Olympia Trading Estate, Coburg Road,
Wood Green, London N22 6TZ

Cover design: Ian Bobb
Cover photography: Ted Taylor

Printed by LPPS Ltd
www.lppsltd.co.uk

British Library Cataloguing-in-Publication Data: a
catalogue record for this book is available from the British
Library

Dedicated to me Mam, me Dad, me brothers, me family and friends.
To me four children (Liam, Calum, Kieran and Kerry).
To Andrea Grainger and Chorlton Bhoy for kind help.
To the Arts Council for financial help when needed.
To Pete Kalu, mentor (tormentor) and friend, who made this book possible.
But especially to Marie who makes it all worthwhile.

For Ali Duff
(1989-2005)
a star still shining.

THE BUTTERFLY THEORY

So how does a drunken gambler land a job in a casino an end up robbin the place? It's a case of the butterfly's wings. You know that idea about how the flap of a butterfly's wings in Malaysia can end up causin a hurricane in Peru? Wid me it all begins when I'm workin as a bonus clerk for the council. I'm responsible for the wages an bonus of thirteen of the biggest pirates Manchester's ever seen, the drivers pool. Then that butterfly's wings flap. Me manager, Mr Tillet has a heart attack an all his work gets shoved on his number two, Caligula (so called cos he's totally fuckin soft). Course, Caligula can't handle the pressure an in typical shit rollin down hill fashion, he pushes more an more my way. All of a sudden it's like the film, *Rio Bravo*, the town drunk is Sheriff.

One of the first jobs Caligula passes down to me is skip tickets. It's basically receipts for the droppin of one load of rubble from a builders skip into the yard of a waste disposal firm. They're redeemable by the company for ninety pound a throw an they come in a pad in triplicate, one signed by the driver, one signed by the skip company, an the third authorised by me for payment.

Soon as Caligula gives me the pad, a thought strikes. The only people who know how many skips per day are emptied are me, the driver an the skip company. The average driver does five a day, but if he was to book nine, who would know? Me fertile mind has soon invented the Imaginary Loads scam. I figure if twenty imaginary skips are booked per week the skip company will be eighteen hundred quid a week better off, with no refuse ter shift or burn. Surely a far sighted businessman would be up for the deal?

At first it's just pie in the sky. Then that butterfly

comes into it again. I visit me brief, Mrs Wesley, an find I'm six hundred quid behind on the drip payments for me divorce. They want money right away or they will have to cease to represent me. I'm gutted. I've got to win the kids, or leastways get decent access. So the Imaginary Loads plan goes live an I trot off to see Joggin Jerry the boss of Waste-Not-Want-Not, a local skip company an breaker's yard.

Jerry's old school.

—Have a drink, he sez, as I walk into his office (which is a leakin Porta-cabin on a croft behind Harpurhey baths).

I have a sharp vodka wid a little coke an no ice.

A little bit of beatin about the bush follows. After about ten minutes Jerry looks at me, bares his immaculate teeth an sez,

—Right! Are you askin me to commit fraud?

An me bottle goes.

—No Jerry, I sez, thinkin a wheel's come off the car an I'm not even out of the pits.

We sit facin each other an I go for it.

—Twenty imaginary loads....eighteen hundred pound....nine for you....nine between me an the driver...an a hundred percent no comebacks.

Another drink passes.

—I've got overheads, he sez.

—Fuck, I sez, —wot overheads? Where yer gonna burn the loads that don't exist?

He smiles.

—Still got business tax an the rest, he sez, —I'll give you six hundred a week.

—An the driver? I ask.

—You pay him out of your share, he sez, —or no deal.

—Seven, I sez, clutchin at rather thin straws.

—Six, he sez in a take-it-or-leave-it tone.

I look him in the eyes. It's a matter of who needs who the most here, an seein as he drives a BMW an I can't afford a car, I think that one's settled.

—Six it is then, I shrug.

I know I'm gettin me hat nailed on wid rusty six inchers but I'm desperate. So I let 'the face that launched a thousand skips' pour me a vodka an coke, an we toast our new business arrangement.

Me next move is to get a skip driver to agree to falsify his tickets an time sheets, commit fraud an risk losin both his livelihood an his liberty, which of course I know won't be hard, but which one? I have basically two choices. Durie or Tucker. Durie is the older of the two an I know him better than Tucker, but I don't like him, so I choose Tucker.

Wham bam a lulu wham bam bam goes Steve Tucker's brain. He needs a job badly because he is due up in court for butting some loser. Steve and Karen were in the Moston Peace Gardens enjoying a drink and this guy was loitering, staring at Karen's arse. He's defiantly stared at least twice at Kazza's mini-skirted rear. Once more, Steve thinks, and he gets it. The guy keeps it up, so that's it, it's head to nose and all over before it's begun. Of course Steve forgot about the CCTV and the police are there in no time. He gets arrested and charged with GBH while the staring guy that started it all gets a hankie and a lift home. There's no justice, Steve thinks.

He's in the shit big time because GBH is a breach of his probation. The shadow of jail darkening his mind, Steve goes and sees his caseworker, McMannus who pulls out all the stops, that is, picks up the phone on his desk, and gets him an interview for a driving job with the council. Steve's got a Class One licence from Haverigg Open Prison where he learnt driving farm equipment.

Steve does a phone interview there and then in the probation office and the council tell him they have jobs set aside for people being rehabilitated and give him a time to come down. He goes for the face-to-face interview, beats off stiff competition from assorted smack heads and glue sniffers and lands the job. He's whistling while he works. It's the best job he's had since the catalogues, and he keeps his head down and doesn't steal too much. Two month later the GBH charge is dropped through lost CPS paperwork. He's free.

Thing is though, Steve likes the job, it's piss simple. What the fuck, he thinks, and he keeps it. Since leaving school, this is his first taste of steady employment. Things are going swimmingly, his repertoire of whistling tunes is expanding, then one day he's walking to clock off and Drunken Duncan out of the office pulls him to one side. Steve has never liked the fucker, never liked the way the Drunk talks in a 'dragged up' style Manchester accent. Sounded put-on to Steve, who himself talks in a 'drugged up' Mancunian style. Something about it made Steve think the Drunk was gay. *I mean workin in an office an with a voice like that*, Steve thinks, *gotta be gay*.

The Drunk pulls on Steve's sleeve, much to Steve's vexation.

—Look, the Drunk says, —I need ter see yer.

Steve looks puzzled.

—What about? he asks.

—Can't say nothin here, Drunk mumbles, —do yer know Billy Green's in Collyhurst?

—Yeah, Steve says, —me dad used to drink in it when it was the Talgarth.

—I'll meet yer in there ternight at half six. An be

alone, Drunk says, and slides away.

Steve's wondering what the fuck that was all about. Then it sort of dawns on him. The Drunk's been staring at him for days. He must fancy him. No fuckin wonder he never docks me when I'm late, thinks Steve.

So Steve clocks off, and fucks off to Karen's on Monsall. He uses his own flat as a giro drop, and as a bolt hole for when Karen hasn't got enough of the white stuff and her moods turn black. His mind's on Karen becaue he's thinking about how Drunk might be in love with him and Karen is in love with him and he definitely prefers Karen, he's not into this man-on-man stuff, a point he's had to emphasise with assorted damage to persons during his various stays in the nick. He goes all misty-eyed as he walks to Karen's, thinking about her.

They met at a bus stop on Ashton Old Road. He was eating some chips, and she was arguing with some bloke over money. Every time the bloke turned his back on her, Karen smiled at Steve. The bloke's maybe six two or six three, but nothing Steve can't handle. Steve stands back, guzzling chips and waiting.

The bloke starts getting a bit rough, pushing Karen against a rail. Steve slings his chips, deciding to intervene. —Leave it out mate, Steve says.

—Wot? the bloke says, turning.

Steve digs two fingers right in his eyes and follows it up with a right cross. An *boom-banga-a bang*, the bloke hits the deck. Steve jumps on his head a bit, then him and Karen jump a 216 into town. They've been together since. And despite its rocky nature, it's been okay, Steve considers.

He gets to Karen's and its fuckin freezin, there's no sign of her and no sign of no tea. There's a stale smell of Stella from last night's cans, which still lie where they were dropped. He decides that they've got to have

9

severe words, —It's getting worse than the last time, he thinks aloud.

He makes beans on toast, adding to the already full sink of pots, and decides he might as well go and see what the Drunk wants.

Billy Green's is about fifteen minute walk from where Karen lives. It's an uneventful walk across Collyhurst Village with nobody about except a few junkies outside the Parkland.

He goes in Billy's. It's empty, apart from Bob Waine and his mates playing cards, and they've been sat in the same chairs since they laid the footings forty year ago.

He orders a pint. From nowhere a voice says,

—I'll get that.

Steve nearly jumps out of his skin.

It's the Drunk.

—Where'd you come from? Steve asks.

—Over there, the Drunk says, pointing to a darkened recess.

—What were yer doin? Steve says, —hidin behind the coat stand?

The Drunk smiles, which Steve don't like, and pays for the beer, which Steve does like.

They head for the recess. Steve's on his guard, *Any funny business*, he thinks, *and he gets it*.

They sit, with the Drunk taking the seat facing the door.

—Look I've got a proposal, the Drunk says.

—You what? Steve says, —be very fuckin careful.

The Drunk hesitates.

—I know how you could make a couple a ton a week widout yer doin anythin, the Drunk says, and waffles on for ten minutes.

Steve can't get his head round it at all, I mean what the fuck is an imaginary load?

The Drunk though, seems to have got it well sussed, and Steve starts seeing pound signs and there seems little to lose. He gulps his pint and makes a decision.

—Okay. I'm in, Steve says, —but if it comes on top you'll be sorry.

They both sit there in silence. Steve's got a few questions but Billy's starts to crowd a bit, and you can't really talk business in a place like this.

—Fancy a can back at mine? Steve asks, adding — and no funny business, I'm straight.

—Only you round here doubtin it, says Drunk, and sniggers at his own remark.

—Strike one, Steve says, —two more and I mangle yer face. But he's smiling as he says it, he's started to like the Drunk.

—I'll get another round, says the Drunk.

Drunk goes to the bar to refresh the glasses, and Steve makes two quick phone calls on his mobile.

First he rings Franco Taxis and asks them to send one post haste to Billy's and make sure not to send the mouthy Scotsman. His second phone call is to Karen.

She answers right away.

—Yeah Babs? she says excited, and Steve knows that she's been for her stuff.

—Listen, Steve says, —doin a bit of business. You in the house now?

—Yeah, she says, —but I'm goin ter bingo wid Chantelle at eight.

—Right, I'm bringin this fella back, says Steve.

She giggles. And Steve gets peeved.

—LISTEN, he says, —this tosser from work's got an idea how to make some money. A couple a ton a week. If you see him don't take the piss, we need him. Gotta go, catch you later, Babs.

Steve hangs up just as the Drunk returns from the

bar.

—Who you ringin? the Drunk asks all paranoid.

—Taxi, Steve says, in a tone that says *you better learn some manners.*

—Oh right, the Drunk says.

And they drink their drink in silence.

I come back from the bar an Steve Tucker's on his mobile. He hangs up an puts it away just as I get ter the table.

—Who yer ringin? I sez, me mind racin through the possibilities.

—Taxi, he replies. His tone unnerves me.

—Oh right, I sez.

The taxi beeps its horn an we drink up an fuck off. Steve jumps in the back ter avoid payin as I get in the front ter give directions to an address I don't know.

—Where to? sez the driver an a notice it's a Scots lad called Tad. He's always a pleasant an chirpy lad. He smiles at me.

From behind Steve shouts the address out. Immediately the atmosphere changes.

—I said I wasn't takin you no more, Tad sez ter Steve.

Steve smiles.

Tad looks at me. I shrug. He don't seem ter wanna drive but he don't seem willin ter try an throw Steve out.

Him an Steve stare at each other.

—You heard the address, jock, sez Steve.

Tad sez somethin under his breath an drives off.

We travel in silence a bit.

—We need cans, sez Steve.

I ask Tad ter run us ter the Derby offy. He does so an I get out an get a carry-out followin Steve's instructions.

We continue in the car in cuttable silence. I know for a fact Tad is completely harmless, which means if Steve can fall out wid him then he's a bit of a loose canon. I'm beginin ter think that maybe doin the scam wid him aint such a good idea after all.

We exit the taxi in Monsall, an I pay.

—Keep the change, Tad, I sez.

He does, but he don't say thanks.

I follow behind Steve, carryin the drink. He gives the door a good clatter, whilst singin, 'I'm comin home I've done my time.'

About a minute later the door opens, an me breath's taken away an me life changes.

I see Karen for the first time.

She's stood there in a purple short nightie thing, her hair tied up like it's just bin washed an on her face is a look that says 'born to fuck'. I'm spellbound. I can't take me eyes off her. She leads us through wid me takin the rear an watchin hers. Steve nips upstairs ter the toilet as I stand at the livin-room door. She walks through to the kitchen, I watch her walkin, so cool an so assured of wot she's doin. I wait for her ter shut the kitchen door but she don't, instead she strips off the nightie. An me gob bounces back off the cheap carpetin. She's still got her back ter me an all she's got on is a light blue pair of knickers, that cover fuck all. I follow the line of her spine from the nape of neck to the swell of her arse an me throat runs dry. An I feel a stirrin in me Wranglers.

I hear a noise on the stairs an I move over ter the other side of the room, an take a chair beneath an empty bird cage.

Steve walks in.

—Want a can? he sez.

—Yeah, I sez thinkin, *why not? I bought em.*

He takes one an throws me one.

—Got a glass? I sez.

—Yer can have an olive an an umbrella if yer want, he sez.

—I'll bring one in, she shouts through. Her voice sounds like rain fallin on a tin roof. It's as Manchester as Mather an Platt's. An a know I'm smitten.

She walks in wearin a short skirt an tiny top. Her entire ensemble could fit in a lucky bag. She walks up ter me wid the glass an a nipple nearly pokes me eye out.

—This is Karen, Steve sez.

I nod.

—An this is Drunk, he sez pointin ter me —I thought he was gay but he's alright. Gonna help make us a good butty.

—How, Babs? says Karen all little girlyish.

An Steve invites me ter tell her. An even though the plan is that only me, Steve an Joggin Jerry can know, I find meself wantin ter impress her an make her laff. An I explain the Imaginary Loads scam from start ter finish, even throwin in additional information about how I intend ter get the skip firm's accounts paid.

Karen gives Bingo a miss an the three of us get pissed. Steve sends Karen out, she comes back wid some chippy an some white stuff. They have a line an the night never seems ter end. As a drift ter sleep in a haze of ganja smoke I'm vaguely aware of Steve singin a varation of *Nights in White Satin* that begins,

'Nights in Miles Plattin...'

The Imaginary Loads takes off an I find little ways of addin to its earnin potential. Within a short time I'm fundin a divorce, a drink habit an I'm gamblin again an Steve an Karen can afford a holiday in Benidorm an a newish Punto.

After seven month of merriment it comes ter a head. The one thing I hadn't accounted for was the drivers' bonus payments. Because of the imaginary loads, Steve is earnin more bonus than the grafters an long term conmen, an he's a new boy. Steve, instead of keepin this ter himself, has openly boasted about it. An Durie, the lad I was originally gonna do the scam wid, goes ter the Union. Durie puts it across that the management are manipulatin the bonus figures. The Union complain ter Management an Management accuse the Union of paranoia. An statements are taken, an books are investigated, an skip tickets checked, an skip companies are visited, an the City Auditors are called in. An Caligula is pensioned off an I'm allowed ter resign an keep me pension an Steve gets sacked an Waste-Not-Want-Not are taken off the suppliers list.

It's the end of the most victimless crime imaginable, the Imaginary Loads (mind, a don't know if the Manchester tenants who dint get their kitchen units renewed that year would agree). I'm on the dole for the first time in me life, an I have ter apply for Legal Aid ter fund me failin divorce. What's worse, me kids have made statements sayin they wish ter remain wid their mam an not reside wid me. It's cos I'm a drunk an can't keep a job, I think. I'm desperate.

I go an see Dr Singh an he gets the Community Alcohol Team people ter do me a home detox. This involves takin away the cold turkey of alcohol withdrawal an replacin it wid the pleasant feelin that Librium brings (they should do one for divorce). The best description I can do of the Librium feelin is that, if someone told yer while yer were on Libby that yer could play the piano, yer'd believe em, an have a pretty good go too. It makes yer wanna love everyone an help everyone.

Then that butterfly's wings flap again. I'm a couple a days on the Librium when Joggin Jerry comes ter see me an thanks me for leavin his name out of it. Jerry does me two favours. He gives me a final payoff for me an Steve, which gives me reason ter visit Steve an leer some more at Karen. An the second favour Jerry does me is ter tell me about a job goin as a receptionist in the Global casino. It's a total come down from plant manager but I let him arrange me an interview cos there aint no other ship on the horizon an if there is then its the H.M.S. Titanic. All said an done, it's a job, an I gotta win back me kids' respect.

So in the middle of me Librium detox I go for me interview at the Global casino.

The Global is situated on the cusp of the Gay Village an Chinatown, in the cellar of a converted warehouse. I arrive fifteen minutes early an I'm bouncin like a Harlem Globe Trotters ball, high as any kite that Mary Poppins ever flew.

I bing-bong the bing-bong an pace round. A can't wait ter get this started so a bin-bong it again an then again. A quite like the tune. I turn ter bing it again an as a do so a man in his early thirties opens the door wid a force unnecessary.

—Ring once an wait, he sez, all surly.

—I've come for the interview, I sez, all smiley.

—Whoopee, he sez an leads me in.

I follow him down the stairs. There's murals on both sides depictin great sportin moments. They blend inter one another, or at least after half-a-dozen Librium they do. The colours an the images fuse an I reach out an touch them. They seem to come alive to my feel. I'm mesmerised as Bobby Moore holdin the world cup fuses inter Lester Piggott winnin a Derby an then metamorphosises inter Jack Nicklaus sinkin a winnin putt.

—Are yer right or wot? shouts me new buddy from the bottom of the stairs.

I'm dragged away from the art exhibition an I dance down the last few stairs.

—Wait there, he sez pointin ter a couple of oxblood couches. I notice his name badge.

—Cheers, Harvey, I sez. He gives me a witherin look.

I start ter read the notices. It's all very upbeat, trips ter the races, fancy dress parties an special nights. I'm gettin excited, it seems a fun place ter work, I might meet the famous an that.

The bing-bong goes. I get up ter answa it but Harvey dashes past me ter get there first. He comes back down the stairs accompanied by a spotty kid aged about nineteen. Harvey points ter the couch next ter me an the kid sits down. Harvey goes back into the casino proper. I'm sat there wid Spotty, so I make conversation.

—Hi, I sez.

—Hi, he sez, an then goes back to organisin his brief case. Shit, he's probably got CV's an certificates in his case, an all I'm holdin is a Racing Post.

—You here for the Reception job? I ask.

—Yes, he ansas an looks the other way.

—So am I, I sez. He turns round ter weigh me up.

—Where yer from?

—Swinton, he sez.

—Long way on the bus, I sez.

—Me dad'll bring me, he sez.

—Still, goin home from here half-four in the

mornin, it's a bit iffy, I sez.

He looks apprehensive. I carry it on.

—Rough round here. The last receptionist got stabbed, I sez, addin —an they call it the Barbary Coast.

A look of shock crosses his face, his idea of the Barbary Coast must be more terrifyin than mine.

—Did he die? he mumbles.

Before I can elaborate on me lie, the door ter the inner-sanctum opens an a woman late forties, but good lookin for her age, comes out.

—May I have James Flynn? she sez, like there's forty of us sat there.

The spotty kid gets up an disappears back inter the casino wid her.

I sit an gaze an think about me interview strategy. I'm lost in thought, mainly about me kids, when Harvey asks, —Coffee or tea?

An before I get time ter answer, the casino door pings open an Spotty flies out an up the stairs widout glancin back.

The woman follows him out, takes one look at me an sez, —I hope you can do nights?

—Seven a week, the Librium sez, answerin for me.

I follow her through the doors. There's this sprawlin, bespangled, glittered, mirrored floor of roulette, card, dice, banco, an marjong tables. My eyes are torn between the golden baubles hangin from the ceiling an the plush maroon carpet beneath me feet. I've entered the gold mines of King Solomon. I was born ter be here, I feel I'm home. I see the ghosts of a thousand gamblers gone, hoverin by the roulette wheels, an the roars of winners echoin round the walls.

I follow the woman through ter this small office, wid one massive decoration, a safe as big as any I've ever seen.

We sit across from each other, her on a swivel chair,

me on a stool type of thing.

—I am Bella Chapman, the senior manager of the Global.

I start ter speak but she interrupts, —Experience? she sez.

—Not as such, I sez.

—Well, what leads you to think you would be an asset to the Company? she sez in a hoity-toity voice.

An that's when the Librium kicked in.

—Well Bella, I began an I ran through every job I've ever had. I explained how I could work as an individual or as part of a team or as both or even be a one man team when the moment demanded. I told her that I was as flexible as Marvo the human tea bag was back before he strained himself an that no shift was a 'no' shift ter me. I said the customers always right an that good manners maketh the man. An that an injustice tolerated anywhere was a threat ter justice everywhere. An at the end of it all I notice a picture of a young girl on the wall. I finish abruptly an sez,

—She yours?

—Yes indeed, sez Bella, all proud —she's my daughter, Glenda.

—Nice kid, I sez.

There's a silence.

—May I confirm you are available for nights? she sez, an we laugh.

So there I am, catapulted by fate (or that butterfly) inter a career as a casino receptionist. I'm attired in black socks, black shoes, black suit, black dickey-bow an white frilly shirt.

In short, I look a right twat.

An I do four straight nights: Wednesday, Thursday,

Friday an Saturday, an finish wid a Sunday day shift. An me divorce ends an the fight for the kids starts an I'm depressed ter fuck. After work I've started callin down at Karen's an Steve's. For eighteen month Karen teases, taunts an tantalises me. Until one night I'm on her couch after a nightshift. I'm pissed up, knackered an dicky-bowed up, an I start rollin a weed. She's braless as usual an me attention is torn between the Moroccan an her nipples. I start to fath about in me head for somethin to say an for some good reason to be starin in her direction. Out of the blue, I announce,

—Hey Kazzer I've got the perfect plan to rob a casino. Its nailed on, can't fail, safe as a premium bond off yer Nana.

She stops pickin dirt from under her toenails. — How much would we get?

—Between sixty grand an a half a million, I sez, exaggeratin, but not by much.

She leans forward. I nearly fall head first into her cleavage.

—Yeah, go on, Drunk, tell me, she sez.

I'm poised there like a hawk above a rabbit, just about to join her on the couch when Steve bursts in.

Karen sez, —Babs, the Drunk's got a plan ter rob a casino.

Steve looks at me intently. Then he sings, 'tell me more, tell me more'.

An I find meself tellin them the first instalment of me plan, leavin out key points cos believe it or believe it not, me plan actually works. Karen's tits are risin an fallin at the twists an contours of the story. Steve's guffawin an gigglin at abduction an abscontion. By the end, even though I only give them a vague outline, they're mewin like kittens wid a ball of wool.

—Can we, Drunk? squeals Karen.

I've got a hard on an I sorta enjoy the attention. Let's have it right, I'm the oldest hat check boy in town. I'm nearly forty an workin on a Reception kowtowin ter all an sundry fer tips an takin rich twats' coats. I come to me senses.

—It's just a story, I sez, dejected, —it aint fuckin real.

—It could be Drunk, you said so, sez Karen.

—We aint got a gun, sez I, puttin a firm stop to the proceedins.

—Who fuckin hasn't? yells Steve. He fucks off upstairs four at a time singin, 'Oh baby let your love run free'.

I'm left starin at Karen's tits. She uncrosses her legs an me eyes are diverted downwards to the previously hidden cache of a thousand wet dreams.

—Go on Drunk, she sez.

An I'm Scooby-Dooless as ter wot exactly she's talkin about.

—Yours if yer want it bad enough, she adds.

But before push can come to shove, Steve's back in the room. An he's carryin wot looks like a pistol. Karen's legs close as me mouth drops open.

—Where? I sez, too stunned ter finish me sentence.

—It's real, screams Kaz.

—I was carriage cleanin on the railway, sez Steve —remember that shootin in Harpurhey, they held up the mini-mart, shot the Vietnamese fella that ran it an made off wid ninety-six quid?

I shake me head.

—Yeah well, he continues, —I seen the lad that done it ditch the gun at the back of some wheelie bins in the acid tubs. So I pulled it out.

—Dint yer burn yer hands? I sez.

—Fuck no, there aint bin acid in em since '98.

—Dint yer tell the Police an that? I sez, almost

ashamed of me naivety.

—Wot for? he sez, puzzled. —Naw they'd of took it......Got four bullets as well, he adds wid pride.

—Three, interupts Karen —we shot that pigeon remember?

—Yeah three, sez Steve.

An there's silence. Me only get-out from The Plan was not havin a gun. In fact I'd never before now seen one. I know if yer live in Manchester yer supposed ter be tooled up an have access to everythin from an Armalite to a Uzi, but it's kinda quiet in Blackley, an anyway I bruise easy.

—Let's do it, sez Kaz.

—Let me think about it, sez I.

—We could torture yer, sez Steve, pointin the gun at me snotter.

Two thirds of us burst out laffin an one third of us nearly has a bowel movement.

—Get me a can, Kaz, I sez.

Karen exits an me an Steve stare at her arse as she leaves. If it wasn't for the want of that I'd be headin for the 17 bus now.

Time ter talk some sense into Strange before Crazy returns.

—Listen Steee........., I start ter say.

—Fuckin jazzin idea Drunk, he sez, —I had yer down as a shitter of bulls but not now.

—No, I sez.

—Wot?

—We gotta think it through, I start ter say as he points the gun. — PUT THE FUCKIN GUN DOWN! I shout.

He puts the gun down, smilin, an I'm relieved ter see I'm still in control.

Kaz returns carryin four Stellas.

—Let's drink to it, she sez.

An I get that sinkin feelin. They're gonna do it with or without me an either way I do time. I shrug me shoulders —First, I sez, —the timin is crucial, gotta do it after a big Saturday.

That's when we take well over a hundred grand.

—How can yer tell a big Saturday? sez Steve.

—When the casino does really well the manager gives us a couple a cans of Boddies ter take home wid us, I sez, slurpin down half a can an starin beyond Steve ter a smilin Karen. An I laugh. —That's right, they make between a hundred grand an a quarter of a mill an me an the croupiers an the valet maids an the rest get two fuckin cans apiece.

As I sez it, I can sense the vainglorious justice of wot we're about ter fuckin do.

I wake up the next mornin, fully clothed on Karen's couch. The coffee table an floor are full of Stella cans so I play find the lady, shake a couple of empties, then spot one on the fireplace an the weight tells me it's half-full. I sip it. I'm not back in work till eight tonight so I settle down for an hour or two.

From nowhere Steve sez, —So we do it Saturday night then?

I drift back into the real world.

—Too many people, I sez.

—But that's when it's codded up wid wedge, he sez.

—Yep, but they don't bank till Monday.

—'Sunday bloody Sunday', he sings.

—An then there's cameras an safes wid timers.

—Yer said yer had a plan, sez he, losin patience a little.

—I have, I sez.

We start drinkin again. I'm sat on the couch an Steve's hoverin over me. I can tell by the movement of his lips that he's thinkin. Karen walks in, Steve's got his back to her. She's wearin a pink kimono with a dragon motif on it. She opens it to reveal the best pair of tits I've ever seen an the smallest thong imaginable. How the fuck did she get in it? I try not to alter me expression, though I suspect it don't work.

She closes the kimono in a flash, plenty of time for me to weigh up her wares but not enough time for Steve to become suspicious.

At this point I'm enjoyin the game.

—Why don't we just do it next fuckin Saturday an take pot luck? sez Steve in a huff.

—Wot an risk everythin for twenty or thirty grand? I sez in a sneery voice.

—Listen to him baby, sez Kaz as she hands me a spliff —he knows wot he's talkin about.

An our hands an eyes engage each other a shade too long.

—No, I sez, —wait till the magic 'two cans'. Once I'm handed them I know there's a hundred grand minimum in that safe an I know it's ours for the takin.

—Right, sez Stevie all business like. —So you turn up here one Sunday mornin about fourish an sez that it's on for later that mornin. But wot the fuck do we do then?

I swig back me warm can an pull on the draw. I gotta give em the meat an drink of The Plan.

—Okay, listen. The Manageress on Saturday night is the same one as on the Sunday afternoon. She does that shift then finishes for her two days off. Her name's Bella. After the Saturday shift Bella'll safe the takins, an on the Sunday she'll come in early to do the float an bag the takins for the bank. Wot I need you two to do is be waitin in her house Sunday mornin when she returns from the night shift at the casino.

—How the fooo......, begins Steve, but I raise me

hand.

—I got the key, I sez, —an she lives in Chadderton. So the second I get out wid me two cans I bell you two, you jump in your Punto an you're waitin in her livin room for her return. Yer've got exactly one hour while she does the count.

—Wot about if some other fucker is stayin over at hers? sez Kaz.

—She's a Bella-no-mates, sez I.

—Where'd yer get the key? An how do yer know it's the right one? she adds.

—Coatboys take coats an hang em up, an Coatboys check pockets an steal an replace. It's her key all right.

—So we got her an we take her back an empty the safe while the casino's empty? sez Kaz.

—Nope, sez I.

—Why the fuck not? sez Steve.

—Cos the safe is on a timer, sez I —an the burglar alarm can't be deactivated till one o'clock on Sunday mornin.

—So wot's the plan, Duncan? sez Kaz an I notice the 'Drunk' label's bin dropped.

—Right you two hold her hostage overnight. Steve takes her to the casino the next mornin. She turns off the burglar alarms an the camera, empties the safe into a briefcase Steve's carryin, leaves with Steve an then she sits alone in a park for three hours before reportin everythin to the police.

They both look at me like I've just come out of Parkhouse.

—An that's it? sez Karen, drawin her kimono as tight as an Italian defence defendin a one nil lead away from home.

—'Doo Wah Diddy, Diddy Dum, Diddy Doo', sez Steve —why the fuck don't she just yell, or signal, or scream or run or a thousand other fuckin things?

—Simple, sez I, an I put the fuckers right in their places, —cos Kaz here has got Bella's fourteen year old daughter tied up an Kaz has got a gun wid three bullets in it. An she emphasises to Mrs Dotin Mother that if she don't obey the orders the kid gets measured for a smaller than normal coffin. An both you an Kaz have got mobiles an if you don't have social intercourse at regular intervals then the kid gets it.

I look across, smilin. There's a look of respect in their eyes that says, the Drunk has thought it through.

—I know Bella well an she only has two loves in her sad life, I continue —her kid an her job. But the job is Beazer League an the kid is Champions League. She cries if the little fucker gets toothache an she still reads her bedtime stories, when she's there. Take me word for it she'll do everythin she's told.

—Yeah but how the fuck yer gonna make her stay in a park for three hours? sez Kaz. I'm realisin that she's the brains amongst 'em.

—Can't be sure that she will cos worry might overcome her, but firstly we give her such a show of force that she daren't risk movin. Second, we take her to Broadhurst playin fields an sit her on a bench, point to a tower block that overlooks it, an sez to her we've a man up there watchin her every movement an if she moves before the three hours is up Steve rings you an you off her little snotter.

It's a vodka moment. Steve pulls three tumblers down from off a cabinet an pours three large vodkas into em an fills em up wid raspberryade.

I look across at Kaz. She seems confused.

—Wot's a matter? I sez.

—How long do I stay alone wid the kid? she sez.

—Ten minutes, I sez, —the second Steve has exited wid Bella you tie up the brat, put tape around her mouth an sling her in the downstairs toilet.

—I dunno, Steve sez, —where the fuck are you while all this is happenin?

—At work, I sez smilin —when you turn up wid Bella I'll be outside waitin for her to open up.

—Won't that look suspicious? sez Steve.

—No kidda, I laugh —that's where I am every Sunday.

They both smile. They're beginin ter get the gist of it. I'll be orchestratin this little concerto from the pits.

There's silence an slurpin an thinkin.

—Yer aint asked the obvious one yet, I sez.

I'm like a teacher tryin ter push his star pupils ter new limits.

They rack their brains but nowt's forthcomin so I help them out.

—How do we get the kid?

—Easy peasy lemon an lime, sez Steve —she's upstairs asleep when we get there.

—Wot a fourteen year old alone in a house at four in the mornin? I sez, —we're talkin Chaddy not Monsall.

—Okay, Big Balls how? he sez.

—Simple. She stays at her dads overnight, I sez, — he drops her off next mornin. Bella an her husband Marco don't talk so he drops the kid at the end of the street. As long as she goes in he don't give a fuck. So that's the first hurdle in the home straight, that kid's gotta walk in that house.

—Has she got a key? sez Kaz.

—Yep but just in case she's forgot her key you leave the fuckin door open.

—Wot if Marco tries ter come in wid her? sez Steve.

—We got three bullets aint we? sez Kaz.

Fuckin hell they're countin bullets now, I'm thinkin, alarm bells ring in me head.

Calm down. This is all hypothetical, I'm just givin

em the synopsis of a novel. I sling down me vodka an raspberry.

—Gotta go, I sez.

Karen walks me to the door which is a first cos normally I just get up an fuck off home. We're stood in the lobby.

—Just think, I sez to Kaz —if the casino job goes right there'll be no more lobbies for us, kid. It'll be halls an vestibules for us after that.

I open me mouth ter laugh but as I do so she presses her lips against mine an me hands grope for her tits. She pulls herself away.

—Come round Wednesday about two, Steve's got Community Service, she sez.

I walk for me bus wid a throbbin head an a throbbin knob.

Wednesday comes an I decide to wear me Wranglers an a leather jacket. Cool but elegant in a Monsall sorta way. I know I'm gonna need an ice breaker so I head for Malik's off licence. As I get there the usual assortment of knobheads are lined up outside. Fourteen an fifteen year old lads wid hair cuts that lobotomy patients used to favour. Young girls wid skirts skimmin their arses.

—Hey you, one of em sez, —get us a Lambrini. I got the one twenty-nine.

—Fuck off, I sez, —you're too young ter ride a motorbike.

—Yer wot? she sez as I shuffle past her an into the shop.

Malik's readin the *Mirror*.

—Bottle of Gordon's, I sez, —an a bottle of Indian tonic water. Do you Indians find it much of a tonic?

He smiles.

—See the BNP took another seat in Burnley? I sez.

—Sadder than sad, he sez, —if things don't improve I'm goin back where I come from. Stockport's got to be better than this.

I take me drink smilin, an bid him farewell.

I get outside an King Knobhead is there. He's about fifteen, a little short-arsed fucker an he's bin givin me grief for about a year.

—Hoy tramp, he sez. I feel the hairs on me head stand on end.

I try to walk on but he's bobbin along at me side.

—Wot's in the bag? he sez.

—Your sister's head, I sez, —now fuck off.

I think I've rode the storm but a figure blocks me path. It's some kid maybe sixteen an he's leanin into me face. He's taller an heavier then me an I feel a little unnerved.

—Got a cig? he sez.

—No.

—Fuckin get one then, he sez. A little shrimp of a girl next to him sniggers.

I dodge round him an walk past the bus stop. Less fuckin hassle if I walk down a stop. I feel cowardly but I know sooner or later these fuckers are gonna have me good style.

I'm twenty yard away an King Knobhead shouts, —Hoy!

I make the mistake of lookin round. —Suck this, he sez, an the scummy little fucker has got his knob out.

—You wanna fuck off home quick son, I shout, —or yer dad'll be first up yer sister again.

It raises a laugh from his mates. I trot on a little faster. An I think to meself that maybe robbin the casino an escapin this purgatory aint such a bad idea.

I jump a 17 down Rochdale Road. It stops ter

change drivers at Queens Park so I get off an walk through to Monsall. I look at me watch. It's five ter two an Steve will be headin off ter Community Service ter decorate old ladies' livin rooms any minute. I'm a bag of nerves. For two year I've dreamt of a carnal carnival with Karen, but now as it nears I'm as shaky as the Oldham Athletic back four. I've had the same packet of condoms in me pocket for six month. I nip inter the Harpurhey Hip to have a quick pint of bitter. Old Ken's there an he's starin at me. I know he's gonna give me the usual load a shit.

—Only three women yer can trust, he shouts, — Me mam, Mother Theresa an Doris Day. The rest is fuckin whores!

I swig long an hard on me pint an gaze again at me watch. Two-ten. I sling the remainder down an walk towards the door.

—Doris Day had more men than the Grand Old Duke of York an he had ten thousand! I shout an exit. An I realise I'm a bigger knobhead than King Knobhead.

I arrive at Kazzer's in a state of giddy apprehension. I give the door a tentative knock. She answers. She's got a duffel coat on. For fuck's sake, I'm thinkin, I was hopin for stockings an supenders.

—Got us a drink, I sez pointin ter the carrier bag as I follow her in.

She's about a couple a foot in front of me an she undoes the toggles on the duffel an lets it drop. *Fuck me, she's naked*. I follow her ter the couch. She turns an sez,

—Yer've got two an a half hours.

—Plenty a time for the drink as well then, sez I, laffin.

I've got her on the couch. She's biting me, first on the lips, then on the ears, then she strips off me shirt an starts on me nipples. Fuck, I think, never got any of this off the ex-wife. I try to reciprocate an bite her lips but only succeed in buttin her on the nose.

She jumps back startled.

—Yer not into any of that violence shit are yer? she asks.

—Accident, I assure her, reachin for the zip of me Wranglers.

The respite gives me chance ter whip down me jeans an shed me duds, an I'm stood there bollock naked apart from a pair of Homer Simpson socks.

As I move over, she leans back an her breasts rise an fall as she stifles a yawn. My mouth locks on her left tit as a wayward finger starts ter penetrate me anus.

'In for a penny in for a pound,' I think an bravely carry on wid the breast chewin.

I've licked, kissed an fondled every part of her body an I'm just about to boldly enter when the phone goes.

—Let the ansa-phone 'ave it, she sez, an I comply.

I'm perched above her when I hear Steve's voice.
—Is the Drunk in or wot? he sez.

Convulsions riddle Kaz's body. I plunge in wid all the finesse of a young Roy Keane.

The voice on the phone continues:

—Can't stay on long, I'm on Tommo's mobile. Let me know will ya, I should be home about....*Fuck off Tommo yer sken eyed cunt I'm talkin to me bird......* Listen I gotta....*Look if yer don't fuck off an plaster that fuckin wall then I'll fuckin plaster you.....*Hi Babs soz about that.....Hang about a second....*Look do yer want a slap?*

The phone goes dead.

I continue wid the buisness at hand. She's got her head trapped against the arm of the couch, one leg over the back an one leg in the ganja tray on the coffee

31

table. I'm thrustin an heavin like a man pushin a wheel barrow up a hill when the phone goes again.

The ansa-phone takes it as I take Karen. It's Steve again.

—Look Babs, give us a ring when yer get back. Don't let the little fucker off the hook.....Hang about.....*I'm a fuckin wot?*......Gotta go, this little tosser... Love ya.

We say nothin an continue wid the job at hand. I'm huffin an a puffin an just about to unleash me load when she sez, —Yer better not pull out. An I just know she's talkin about the casino job.

—Consider this a small deposit, I sez.

An I come in a blaze of glory an she kicks the ganja tray onto the carpet.

I extricate meself from her an start ter pick up the ganja an papers an wot have yer. Somehow the biscuit barrel's got tipped over an can I fuck tell the Moroccan from the ginger snap. An I just know I'm gonna end up smokin Jammie Dodger.

I sit back down, pour meself a treble gin an her a good double, an think about me predicament while playin wid an extended nipple.

—He'd kill you if he found out, she sez.

—He won't find out, I sez. An she smiles.

An I realise I'm in it right up ter me gonads. He's strange, she's crazy an I'm bein ruled by me prick.

THE BIG WHEEL OF LIFE

An there it all may have ended but about a month later an array of circumstances pushed me from a mood of apathy into a *couldn't give a fuck* mood. Yer may be wonderin wot the difference is but believe me there's a world.

On the Saturday I'm walkin down Portland Street, I'm in plenty of time for work so I duck in the Monkey an sits down next to Chinaman. Let me tell yer about Chinaman. He aint Chinese, he's from Miles Plattin an his real name is Billy Kelly. But a couple of year back he had a stroke an then a couple of months later he had another stroke. So the lads in the pub nickname him 'the speakin clock'...cos 'at the third stoke' an all that. Then Billy got a urine infection an was nippin ter the bog every five minutes so his nom de plume got amended to 'the leakin cock' which some smartarse thought sounded Chinese. So Billy there on in became known as the Chinaman. Anyway, the Chinaman tells me about somethin he's seen on telly the night before.

—Did yer see that thing about parasites last night? he sez.

—Fuck off China, I sez, —I drink with enough parasites without watchin em on telly.

—No, listen Drunk, he sez, —ever hear of Sleepin Sickness?

—Yeah, sort of, I sez.

—Well I seen this thing, right? Some kid gets bit by this bug thing. An it burrows itself inter his skin. An he lives in a village in Uganda an his mam an dad take him to hospital. An it's Sleepin Sickness that he's got. An he's nine. An they've caught it early. An he don't have to die.

—Hooray for Hollywood, I sez.

—Yer not listenin, sez he all irate —they tell the

kids parents that for 20,000 Ugandan shillins their son can live. An the parents aint got that kind a money. So they take him home. An the bug gets to the kid's brain. An bingo, he's dead a fortnight later.

Silence. I look at Billy.

—Fuck Billy, I sez, —I've gotta do a nightshift in an hour, give us a break.

He grabs me arm, an if I didn't know the old thief better I'd swear he's near ter tears.

—Yer know how much 20,000 Ugandan shillins is? he sez.

—No, I sez.

—Six fuckin quid, he sez, —for that pissin amount some kid has ter die.

He finishes his pint an fucks off. An I'm left there shell shocked. Wot the fuck does he want me ter do?

I go in work. Me head's wrecked. I'm goin through a bad divorce. I see me football team more often than I see me kids an I don't go to the matches that much anymore. An for some reason I can't get the thought of that kid dyin for the sake of six quid out of me mind.

I get in an it's a slow night. Let me tell yer about casinos. They're usually situated downstairs with no windas an no clocks an no concept of time. They're murky, tacky an cheap, with customers ter match, an the management run em like detention centres.

I'm sat there readin, takin coats an checkin people in. It's the usual shower of shite comin down the stairs. I'm workin wid Colin. He's a decent lad who only gives a fuck about football, so I shake me mood off an get engrossed in *Candide*. I don't hear the door *bing bong* the entrance of the biggest arsehole the casino has amongst its membership, a famous Manchester barrister by the name of Norris McCoyle. He's defended em all, has our Norris, every codded ter the gills abuser an user that can afford ter pay his inflated charges. An he's got most of em off.

I look up ter see his drink sodden face an note the new whore who's keepin him company. I put me book down, —Lovely night, Mr McCoyle, I sez, —can I take the lady's coat?

She shuffles out of her month's earnins an he takes it from her shoulders an hands it to me. I don't give him a ticket cos the tosser always slings em.

—WHAA? he sorta says, —yours? He picks up me book.

—Yeah, I sez, an I note his grin.

He points to the cover an motions to his female guest as I open the guest book for her ter sign.

—Strawberries for donkeys, he sez. She breaks into a laugh.

I'm annoyed. —You read it? I ask, an he looks taken aback. A lackey has broken the rules.

—Yes, at University, he answers.

—Oh I have the advantage then, I sez, —I read it for fun an not cos I was instructed to.

There's a silence. McCoyle is a big player. Some nights he drops ten grand at Roulette an another ten at Blackjack. It don't pay ter smack his arse with his own weapons.

He says somethin but I don't quite catch it.

—Have a nice evenin, I sez, an press the buzzer for entry an gesticulate wid me free hand.

—Fucking hell, Drunk, sez Colin —did you see the tosser's face?

—Serves him fuckin right, I sez.

I'm made up an I get on wid me job.

An old Chinese girl comes down the stairs. She's wid Missy Lee, 869, funny how yer memorise punters' numbers.

—Missy Lee friend must 'chin may' (sign in), I sez, an then we go through the entire pantomime.

—'Cheesing', Missy Lee's mate sez.

It means 'fool'. I smile an sez —'Day Gee-A' (address), an she complies.

So I sez, —'Dojay' (thankyou), an they fuck off inside.

About an hour later, Bella the Manageress comes out an she's fumin —Exactly what did you say to Mister McCoyle? she sez.

I shrug.

—I've just had to give him and his lady friend a complimentary meal. Moreover, he's bent my ear for an hour regarding lack of respect. Henceforth, you will keep your big mouth tightly shut. And when he leaves, you will apologise. Understand?

I look at her.

—Wot for? I sez.

An she loses it.

—Because I am ordering you to and that's reason enough!

Colin shuffles about embarrassed. She's sacked people for less.

—Who in heavens do you think you are? she sez.

I've seen these belittlin tactics before. She's got a bucket full of men's balls in her office. I'm lookin at her stood beneath me. I'm breathin heavy. She still aint finished.

—Have you been drinking? she says, an I know it's a sendin home offence.

I'm in two minds ter tell her ter stick her poxy fuckin job. But I fuckin need it. Wot a fuckin life. —Look Bella......, I start ter say, but she's havin none of it.

—Apologise and make it good. And no more wisecracks. One more drink before coming on duty and your scrawny arse won't touch. Understand?

She stares in me eyes. I'm thinkin *fuckin bitch...that bastard in there can sez wot he likes ter me an I gotta wipe his arse.* An the injustice of it all. I can only see me kids wid a chaperone if I step out of line one more time. I gotta take shitty coats in a casino ter pay the CSA. An this woman ten year me junior gets ter talk ter me like I'm nothing.

—Earth to cretin, come in cretin, over, she sez.

An I remember Steve's gun. An I'm in. This place gets turned over an I don't give a flyin fuck.

—Sorry Bella, I sez, —had a bad day thinkin about the kids.

—No shit, I've had a bad life. Your very last chance, she sez. She marches back through the doors an into the casino.

Colin looks at me. I've got tears in me eyes. It's hard ter explain, fuck all ter do wid wot she's just said, more ter do wid some fuckin Ugandan kid. I pull meself tergether, but that's it, me minds made up, the next Saturday that the casino has a good night, then Bella fuckin don't.

First thing next mornin I'm clatterin at Kazzer's door.

—Who the fuck is it? shouts Steve as he lumbers down the stairs.

—Avon wid attitude, I sez an rap out 'you're gonna get your fuckin head kicked in' on the knocker.

Steve opens the door stark bollock naked.

—'Hey big spender spend a little time wid me', he sings an throws the door wide open.

He walks inside, his fat arse wobblin side ter side. I follow, shakin me head.

—Put some fuckin clothes on, I sez, —nude day's Tuesday.

He puts on one of Karen's nightgowns. It's pink an too short for her, let alone him.

—Wot yer want? he sez.

—Got any drink? I enquire.

—Some vodka under the sink an some cherryade in the fridge, he sez, lightin a tea stained fag that he finds on the coffee table.

I go ter get meself a mix.

—Not seen yer for a while yer shite-hawk, he sez.

—Busy, I sez, —you still got the gun?

—Why? Wanna do a Brinks Matt?

—The casino is on for a week on Saturday, I sez.

He jumps up, so does his tackle.

—Ste, put some fuckin clothes on, will yer?

He goes upstairs, passin Karen as he does.

—Wot yer want? she sez, an I'm gettin dizzy on the deja-vu.

—Casino, week Saturday, I sez, —you in or wot?

She smiles. —Thought yer'd pulled out, she sez.

—Never do, sez I.

I wait while Steve comes downstairs.

—Okay, he sez as he re-enters the room with clothes on —wot's the crack?

—Chinese Mooncake day, I sez.

—Yer wot?

—It's a big Chinese celebration, a bit like Valentines Day.

—Is mooncake drugs? asks Karen.

So I explain.

—It's a sort a fable, like Cinderella. There's this Moon God an he falls in love wid this Sun God, but her parents don't wanna know. So the only way they can pass messages is inside these cake thingys. An once a year the Chinese have *Mooncake Day* an yer give everyone these fuckin horrible cakes. Sour egg in oil in a kinda pastry. I ate one last year, Morgan Ho gave it me, I puked it right back up.

—Yer losin me, sez Kaz.

—The casino is havin a party ter celebrate it a week on Saturday. The Chinese will be comin from as far as Birminham. Anyone who's anyone in the Chinese community will be in the casino that night, an codded up ter the gills. The casino'll make at least a quarter of a million. That money sits in the safe till Sunday mornin. Now no more fuckin about. Are yer in or are yer out?

—'My, my, my, Delilah', laughs Strange.

Karen's noddin an pullin on a Benson.

An the party starts in earnest. I'm sat between em on the couch. The music's blarin away so we have ter shout above it ter be heard.

—Have yer got enough for another bottle of vod? Steve enquires of Kaz.

—Yeah, no probs, she sez, —I'll take it out of your fine money. We won't be strugglin for that after Saturday week.

We're all laffin so I decide ter tell em the bit I bin dreadin.

—We need a fourth includin, I sez.

—Who an wot fuckin for? asks Kaz.

—Well, I continue, —you two got a quarter of a million in a bag while I'm stuck at the casino gettin interviewed by the police. Wot's ter say yer don't do a runner wid my share?

They look genuinely hurt.

—Wot I want is some sorta collateral, I sez, —I want you ter give me your passports, an I'm gonna give em someone ter mind. That way if you don't show up wid my share, at the address I give, then they get sent ter the Police.

—Fuckin hell, Drunk, yells Steve —you'd grass?

—Would I fuck, I sez, —cos you two aint gonna do a fuckin runner, are yer?

—Who though? Steve asks.

—Billy the Chinaman, I sez.

—He's fuckin mad, sez Crazy Karen.

I shrug. —Yeah, but he's trustworthy.

They don't look too sure, so I play me ace. —I pay the Chinaman out a my share, I sez.

—Only fair, sez Steve —it's you that don't trust us.

Karen gives Steve the vodka money an he shoots round ter Moorsey's for a bottle of Monsall's finest.

Meanwhile me and Karen sit across from each other.

—Yer not bin back for more, she sez.

—When's he back at Community Service? I sez. I'm like some Blackpool magnet an she's me fridge (an frost free at that).

—He's cleanin the graffiti off the shops on Wednesday. But it's risky cos he usually makes Thommo do it an sneaks home here for a fuck. He's in court Monday for TDA if yer fancy it then? she sez.

—Wot happens if he gets time on Monday? I sez, concerned that our plan is gettin scuppered before it's started.

—Just up for pleadin, she sez, —an he's pleadin not guilty.

—Monday it is then, I sez an I walk over an twitch the curtains.

No fucker's in sight so I whip me knob out an she begins ter polish it. I'm just about ter see the pyramids across the Nile when Steve walks round the corner carryin a bottle of Monsalloffski. An he's with Kilkenny Benny.

I sit down an pretend ter be readin last week's *News of the World*.

They walk in an I let on ter Benny. —Alright yer peg pushin bastard? I sez by way of greetin.

—Yeah, sez he, grinnin like a lottery winner.

—Tell the Drunk about Saturday, sez Steve.

He tells me this story bout pickin up this tramp in London while they was comin back from a match an droppin him off in Victoria Manchester instead of Victoria London. As he finishes there's tears rollin down his face an I'm laffin me fuckin bollocks off.

—Fuckin football, hey? Kilkenny Benny sez.

An for the first time in a long while I'm relaxed. I aint screwin me head up worryin about me ex-wife an me ex-kids, or Ugandans wid Sleepin Sickness or psychopathic teenagers hangin round off licences ready ter kick the shite out of me. An I have a good feelin about the robbery. Now all I gotta do is find the Chinaman an offer him two grand ter mind some money for me till the heat dies down.

I go ter Miles Plattin on a lieu day. It's Friday, eight days before the job, an I gotta find the Chinaman. I first try his flat in Albert Court, number 56 on the eleventh floor. I knock like fuck but get septic knuckles. A door opposite opens an a woman peers out.

—Benefit day son, she sez, —he'll be in the pub.

—Cheers, I sez.

I head for the Spankin Rodger, but the place is empty. Then I get a bit of luck. I bump into Scots John in Ladbrokes opposite the Playhouse. I've known this slime ball thirty year an I know that if he finds out that I'm desperate ter find the Chinaman then just for the sake of bein a cunt I won't get nothin out of him. So I play it cagey.

—Right Johnboy? I say, —backin em all?

He snorts an I take a bettin slip.

—Fuckin pubs round here are dead, I sez.

—You're no kiddin, he sez, —better in the town. Cheaper too.

—Bus fare though in it? I sez.

—Gorra bus pass, he sez.

—How'd yer get one of them? I ask.

—Easy, he sez, —I'm an alcoholic an I got it so's ah can attend mah meetins.

—You as well? Billy Kelly is too, I sez, studyin the card at Fakenham.

—Reminds me of the ex-wife that does Fakenham, he sez, —that's wot she was good at when it came tae orgasms.

I laugh along.

—Aye Billy, he's same as me, attended ten meetins, got his free bus pass an now drinks in Sasha's, 99p a pint. Better than round here, an they got paid artists as well. Last week Jackie 'The Boss' Ross was on doin Elvis, an this week...

I'm off.

—You no havin a flutter? he asks.

I get ter Sasha's an it's hammered. Wall ter wall drunks availin themselves of a happy hour that lasts all day. It's four deep at the bar, a real dipper's delight. The ashtrays aint bin emptied since the last time I was in. Happy Hour. I look around me. Not a smiley face for love nor money. Just the beaten, forsaken look of losers.

Some old girl starts slaggin her man off. Judgin by the state of his shirt he is the proud owner of one broken iron. He's tryin ter calm things but she aint havin none of it.

—Wot yer fuckin go back for then? she screams.

—Me National Insurance card, he sez.

—Lyin fuckin bastard, she sez, —yer went with her, dint yer?

—Pet she's not a patch on you, he declares, tryin ter put an arm round her.

Amid it all I spot the Chinaman, nursin a pint. He's at the bar sat on a stool.

—Billy me old China, I dive over an sez, —am I glad ter see you. Drink?

He looks confused.

—Bitter? I sez.

—Who wouldn't be? sez he.

—Gotta proposition for yer, I sez as I order two pints of bitter.

It erupts between the arguin couple. She kicks her chair back, slings a pint over lover boy, an storms out into Oldham street. He pockets her cigarettes an lighter an chases out after her shoutin, —Pet, nothin happened!

Someone on the table behind takes the departed man's half drunk pint an returns to his own table.

—Let's grab the table, I sez ter Billy, movin off fast ter make sure I get the dry seat. We get sat down.

—Before we start, he sez, —I don't wanna buy nowt or try nowt. Yer can buy me beer all day long but you've fuck all I want, so there's fuck all I can do for yer.

—If I gave yer two grand for doin fuck all wot would yer do wid it? I sez.

—A Polish man who'd lived fifty year in America was asked if livin there had taught him anythin, he sez, starin at his pint.

—And? I enquire.

—He replied that he had learnt that there was no such thing as a free dinner. An I sez ter you now Drunk, there's no such thing as a free dinner.

—Two grand Billy saves a lot a kids' lives in Uganda, I sez, —now do yer wanna listen an learn or do I fuck off an find someone less drunk an more reliable?

—I'm listenin, he sez.

—Next Sunday someone's gonna bring yer a bag wid money in it, I sez, —an your gonna mind it for me till it's safe for me ter collect it. In a separate envelope will be two grand for you.

—Who brings the wedge? he sez.

I gulp down a part of me pint, smile an sez, —Karen an Steve.

—Aw ter fuck an back, she's fuckin crazy, he sez, shakin his head.

—Yeah? She reckons you're mad, I sez in retaliation.

—You fuckin her? he sez.

—No fuckin way, I sez.

—You fuckin idiot, he sez, still shakin his head

—Keep yer head still will yer? I sez, —in or out? Simple question.

—Nobody gets hurt. No violence. Understand? he sez.

—Yeah, I sez.

An we sit back each lost in our thoughts.

—Fuckin great this, he sez, laffin —she's crazy, I'm mad, an Steve's fuckin strange.

—An I'm fuckin depressed, I sez, breakin into a grin.

—Okay, he sez, —I'll do it. Yer know why?

—Money? I sez.

—No, he sez, —cos I'm a thief, it's me nature. That's why I'll do it, Drunk.

An we have a beltin drink in all the cheap price places of wot our useless Labour Council have dubbed the Northern Quarter, finishin round about midnight outside the Frog an Bucket. By then we're both as pissed as Apaches at a rain dance. I'm holdin him up an tryin ter navigate him across an empty road. I finally get him ter the bus stop outside the Big Issue, though fuck knows what month the next bus is due.

—Get a taxi? I sez.

—Fuck off, he sez, —not made a money.

—I'll pay, I sez. After all, I'll soon be rich.

—Don't want no charity, he sez.

Which would be an admirable sentiment if of course Billy hadn't had lived on charity all his fuckin life.

He unwraps his supper, a kebab he bought from the Radgar on Oak street. Looks the fuckin part as well, I'm sorry I dint get one now.

—Ever done time? he asks.

—No, I answer, surprised at the question.

—Thought not, he sez smilin, —still time though.

I stand lookin at him, swayin. Or maybe he's stood still an I'm swayin, it's hard ter tell.

—Look Billy, I sez, —get a taxi. I bung a fiver in his jacket pocket.

—Naw, he sez, —off ter do a fanny count in fook finders. You up for it?

—Not for me, I sez.

An he smiles.

—You're keepin bad company, he sez.

—You aint that bad, I laugh.

An I turn an stroll up the road wid the strains of his voice behind me singin,

'When I was young an lazy
as lazy as can be
I said goodbye to the mother-in-law
an off I went ter Sea...'

The clock of life skips on an it's Monday an I got me date wid Kaz. I gotta get meself ready an get me head sorted. Me stomach's churnin from too much cheap beer yesterday an gettin too near the robbery. So I take an alka-seltzer an a weed then sit in me livin room an gaze out me winda at the avenue in the rain. I go over ter the picture of me kids on the windasill. Every mornin I wish em good mornin an that. I pick it up.

—Right, you four, I sez, —get a move on or you'll be late for school.

They smile back at me, they always smile back at me.

I'm feelin a bit groggy so I get meself a small bowl of cornflakes. I chomp em down, an fight the urge ter bring em right back up again.

I look around me flat. I left the matrimonial home wid two black bin bags full of clothes, an nothin else, not even dignity. The furniture here's mainly stuff given to me by mates, an a fuck-off big telly that I bought in the auctions. I like me telly. I pick up an ornament, it's somethin me youngest Eammon got me from Blackpool, a cup that sez 'To the best Dad in the world' on it. The world's changed a lot since he bought me that, I think ter meself.

I take a swig on me cold coffee an mull things over. It's less than a week away from robbin the casino. There's two things on the immediate agenda. First, I knock the back out of Karen, an second I see me kids before the big event. Let's have it right, if we fuck up on this, me seven year old will be thirty by the time I get ter see her again. So I pluck up the courage an I ring the former matrimonial home. The ansa-phone kicks in:

—Hello this is Debbie speakin I'm not in at the moment. But if you leave your name and number I will get back to you as soon as I possibly can.

I start laffin. Half ter show her that I don't care an half cos of nerves.

—Fuck me, Debbie, I sez, —that's the nicest yer've ever talked ter me. If yer after a reconciliation yer can fuckin...........

An she picks it up, don't she. —Wot? she sez.

—I'd like ter see the kids, I sez.

—Study the court papers, she sez.

—No listen, I start ter say.

—No you fuckin listen, she interjects, —if yer come anywhere near this fuckin door I'll have the Dirty here in five fuckin minutes. Understand?

—Please, I'm off the beer an I just wanna take em out on Thursday.

—You're off fuck all apart from yer head, she sez.

An I laugh, an it's daft but she does too.

—Listen, I got a joke, I sez.

—Aw don't, Duncan, she sez.

—No listen, I sez, —Macca told it me.

—How is he? she sez.

She always liked Macca but when Macca found out that she'd shit on me he vowed never ter speak to her again. An he hasn't.

—Mad as snot, I sez.

—Look if yer have em Thursday, wot time do yer pick em up an wot time do I get em back? If it's like last time there'll be no next time.

—Jesus, Debbie we didn't need Relate, we needed Victim Support, I sez.

—Wot fuckin time? she sez.

—Nine till seven, I sez.

—Nine till five, she sez.

—I'll see your five an raise it one.

—Yer not funny, she sez, gigglin.

—Wanna hear Macca's joke? I sez.

—No, she sez. —Thursday at nine then?

Yeah, I sez, —I'll give yer a knock.

—No, she sez, —I'll send em to yer. Yer not allowed near this door.

An I think about the fuckin door I aint allowed near. I stole that fuckin door, now I can't come fuckin near it. Seems she got custody of that as well.

—Okay, I sez, —taxi em to me. Same as usual I'll

be outside the Lion an Lamb.

—Make sure it is outside an not inside, she sez in a tired voice, —that taxi firm think I'm as bad as you are.

—Yer got a good case for suin, girl, I sez, —get on ter Mrs Goodwin.

Mrs Goodwin was her solicitor in Drunk v Mrs Drunk, our divorce case. The girl who said that I put my vodka in the kids' Calpol, when in effect I put the kids' Calpol in my vodka. There's a difference, see: the first one implies that I did it for the children ter drink an that would be child cruelty, whereas the second tells the truth, it was an alcoholic experiment. An believe it or not it don't taste as bad as it sounds.

—Right, bye, she sez.

An the phone goes dead.

So now I gotta book Thursday as a holiday. But I got me thinkin cap on. The kids are on a school holiday, so me bookin a day off from work looks like somethin a normal dad would do. If the Dirty check it out it'll all ring true.

Monday comes an I come.

I'm lay on the couch afterwards, wid her lyin across me, her head on me arm. I look around at me surroundins. There's the brown couch an two different shade of green chairs. An empty bird cage hangs above an unplugged lava lamp which is holdin centre stage on top of a massive telly. I count three tellys.

—Why three tellys? I ask.

—Two's broke, she sez, as if I've asked a stupid question.

—Right, I sez.

She's got a strange look in her eyes. She appears ter be in a state of bliss. Takes all sorts, I think.

—You like it here? I ask.

—It's okay, she sez.

She shuffles up me body an comes ter rest on me chest.

An I weigh her up. In a different place, in different company, wid better luck, she coulda bin a model or a movie star. I kid yer not she's got beautiful colourin, sorta Brazilian, wid dark long hair, a pert mouth an cheeky smile. An eyes a man could kill for, forget his name or jump off a winda-sill for. An somethin strikes me about Karen, I aint never seen her wid make-up on, I aint never seen her wid designer clothes on, aint never seen her in a pub beyond Monsall, an yet I aint seen no girl ever that looked as sexy as she does widout even tryin.

—Why don't yer throw away the tellys that don't work? I ask.

—He'd only bring in other junk if I did, she sez, laffin.

—Where's he get it all from? I ask, bewildered.

—Old habits die hard, she laughs, —once a skip man always a skip man.

—I'd bin the fuckin lot, I sez.

She just shrugs; the junk is part of her world in more ways than one.

Its bin a hard mornin shaggin an a check me watch. I better get me things tergether an head up Rochdale Road, I think.

—Roll us a weed, sez Karen.

For her, anythin. I go about the business of makin a joint, a skill first learnt at school. Silently an diligently tearin the Rizla papers an lickin them into place. Lovingly burnin the weed into the tobacco, before twirlin it an rollin it. She watches, a tea stained eiderdown for a blanket. I rip the cover of the Rizlas for a roach. She halts me in mid rip.

49

—Fuck me, she sez, —how big yer gonna make that roach?

—Wot? I sez.

—Get fuckin cardboard poisonin from that thing, she sez, an leans over, laffin at her own joke.

The eiderdown drops from her tits, an I notice their perfect symmetry.

I bite off the tip of the weed, spit it out, an draw deep.

She's hoverin like a buzzard over a dyin rabbit. I pass her the smoke. She's made up.   —You wanna hear how I lost me virginity? she sez.

Before I can sez, 'if I must', she's tellin me. I sit back an listen an try not to interrupt:

—I was fourteen an did it with me dad's best mate for a jar of Uncle Joe's Mint Balls. It was one Sunday dinner, me dad comes back from the pub. Fuck all on telly in them days so the old man an Rodger the lodger, his mate, get the Davenports out. It was this beer at home shite that yer sent off for. They used ter sit there singin the silly song off the advert an playin imaginary drums an trumpets ter accompany 'emselves. Ter be honest it was nice ter see me dad happy, so I sung along wid em. I was always allowed one glass of beer, an me mam had a shandy.

Anyway this one day me dad an Rodger get back from the pub an Rodger's won a big jar of Uncle Joe's Mint Balls on the name card in the Grey Mare. The tosser won't open em an he starts tormentin me wid em:

—Go on, I sez, —give us some.

—Savin em, he sez.

An I'm gutted. I know that he aint got no one ter save em for, cos his common-law has run off wid a van driver from Gorton.

So they hammer their barrel an me dad falls asleep. Soon after, me mam fucks off ter bingo. I'm sat there an Rodger's starin at me. I might be a virgin but I aint daft. I've had a good many a gropin off the van boys at the mill an earned a few bob, so I know how many beans make five.

—Go on, I sez, —give us the Uncle Joes.

As I sez it I stretch an me tits nearly come out of me blouse.

—Wot's in it for me? he sez, leerin.

I'm lyin on the carpet so I sorta uncross me legs an sez —don't know wot yer mean.

That's it then. His eyes are poppin out of his head an he motions me into the kitchen. Me dad's well away on the couch an Rodgers walkin like a tripod. I remember him sayin he was hung like a donkey an that his wife couldn't handle the size of it. He gets me in the kitchen. His hands are everywhere. I'm thinkin I've earned half the jar already. We had one of them servin hatches for passin food through an the doors have bin taken off, so I'm in direct view of me dad if he wakes up from his siesta.

Anyway, he gets me over the fridge which is directly under the hatch an as he grabs me, me dad's dinner goes flyin. I'm still hagglin, —Wot do I get? I sez, one hand holdin me knickers up an the other tryin ter keep him at bay.

He's frantic by now.

—The whole fuckin jar, he shouts, an nearly wakes me dad up.

I'm happy wid the deal. He whips out his park railin. I'm thinkin, aren't donkeys small? I turn round an next thing yer know I'm bein well an truly Rodgered, six feet away from me dad, who's snorin an totally impervious to the deflowerin of his daughter by his best mate.

—Yer know, she sez, —lots of girls say it hurts first time but I took to it, me, an we were at it like knives whenever we could. The obvious happened, she concludes, —me dad caught him givin me a good seein to on the back verandah. He punched Rodger's face in an then kicked him out.

She draws on the weed, giggles an sez, —You know what, Drunk? Ter this day I can't suck an Uncle Joe widout gettin randy.

I'm lyin there, me knob achin hard, strokin her. I'm just about ready to open the second innings when she sez out of the blue,

—I fuckin hated me dad, he used ter batter me mam shitless.

I try playin with her right nipple but she's oblivious, carryin on with her story, so I give up an listen:

—He'd wait while she come home an he'd make her make the tea an then he'd throw it at the wall. Then he'd start askin her about other men. I remember this one time, mam's bin away for about four days, an he'd searched everywhere for her. He'd got it in his head that she was wid some fella but she was in a battered wives hostel. Anyways he goes out an buys this record, *Hello Dolly* it was called. An he plays it over an over. An about two days later she sneaks home ter see us an he catches her. At first he talks nice to her. Then he grabs her by the hair an he walks her into a mirror, not up to a mirror yer understand, fuckin into one. Her blood is goin everywhere. She's screamin 'Not in front of the kids!'.

—Bastard, I sez.

—An me brother, Ken, she sez, —tried ter get in between them, an me dad backhanded him an broke his jaw. He had ter have it wired up an eat through a straw for a month. I was lyin near the door cryin. I'd always bin Daddy's Little Princess. He came over ter me an he kicked me legs an shouted, 'whore, just like yer fuckin mother!' I was only nine. He marched me mam round the room slappin an kickin her, that fuckin record playin over an over an over again, 'Dolly don't yer ever go away again'.

When he died I spat on him in the coffin. Yer know wot the undertaker said?

—No, I sez.

—He said, she recalls, laffin, 'grief affects people in different ways'.

I let out a long sigh. This girl is as crazy as they get.

—Shit, I sez, lookin at me watch —I gotta get movin.

Her mood swings again an she grabs me by me wilted weapon an sez, —Tell me how you lost your virginity.

—Well, I sez, —it was to Noddy Holder.

An before I can explain that it was whilst listenin to Noddy an not havin carnal knowledge of Noddy, she's on me.

—Yer dirty little fucker, she laffs, —tell me all about it.

I'm stood outside the Lion an Lamb. The kids' taxi's late. I start pacin up an down an gettin angry. Nine a fookin clock means nine a fookin clock, not quarter ter ten. She does it every time, just ter show me who's boss, just ter grind me snotter a little further inter the dog shit. Wasn't always like this though. One time she doted on me. Somewhere in there I killed it all off, drilled a little hole in her heart an siphoned off all the love. An I think of the little things, an maybe they weren't so little. I remember her barrister rippin me to pieces in court, over one of Debbie's suicide notes. She'd took an overdose an left a 'goodbye cruel world' letter, only to wake an find I'd corrected the grammar an marked it, '4/10. Must try harder'.

An I think about the time all those dreams ago when it was me an her against the world. An this one occasion comes ter mind. We were up to our eyeballs in debt, though when I sez we, I really just mean me. Everybody seemed to be queuin up to knock us down. We owed a debt collector called Ferris six hundred, an he'd decided that the waitin game was over. I'd bin given till Wednesday to pay up or face the consequences, an the consequences weren't no county court summons. The last reneger that Ferris had 'Wednesdayed' had got taken to Barney's Tip, stripped naked, had petrol poured over him, his manhood laughed at an then threatened with a lit match. So not payin was not a good idea.

We also had a council tax bailiff comin for five hundred on Wednesday as well. The only happy thought on the horizon was Ferris's men gettin me an the bailiff mixed up an him accidentally gettin Wicker-manned on Barney's Tip instead of me.

I had ter get me hands on eleven hundred pound pronto. I borrowed off every fucker I knew, an all I could raise was £500. In a fit of panic I took Debbie down to Mays pawnshop on Collyhurst Street, an she hocked all her jewellery. Which raised a paltry ton. So there was nothin for it but put it all on a horse. Six hundred ter win.

It's Cheltenham Gold Cup Day, an me an Debbie are outside Bosworth Brothers bookies, an we're rowin like fuck.

—No fuckin way, she's sayin.

—Yes fuckin way, I'm sayin, —the lot on Dawn Run.

—Bad ter fuckin worse, she's sayin. The two little ones (we only had a brace a kids at the time) are in the double trolley cooin an mumblin ter each other.

She relents: —How much back if it wins?

—If we do the favourite, nearly two grand, I sez, —enough ter pay everythin an get your rings out before the ink's dry on the pledge.

—Wot about the rest? she sez.

—Get yer somethin, I sez, —an a bit for the kids. An a holiday an that.

She's thinkin about it but there's no other way forward. I take a hold of Brendan an carry him in, only for some fat fuckin jobsworth ter say,

—Gotta be 18.

I take Brendan back to his mam, an prop the bookies door open.

—Wot if it loses? she sez, all worried.

—It won't, I sez.

She goes to open her mouth but I stop her with a kiss.

—Don't worry, I sez, —this is the turnin point.

—More like you'll finish up in Turnin Point, she sez, in a battle weary voice.

I go over to the telly on the wall an read 'Dawn Run 9/4'. I walk back out.

—Do or die, I sez, puttin the decision on her toes.

She shrugs an bunches up the blanket on the babies. I take this as a yes, an walk back in.

I take up a slip, write '£600 win Dawn Run 9/4', walk to the counter an give the fat girl the bettin slip. She looks at me wid renewed respect. Inside, me heart's beatin an me arse is twitchin, but on the outside I'm as loose as a goose.

—Just have ter check this with the manager, she says, an wanders over to him.

He looks at the bet an at me an then back at the

bet, an just as he's noddin ter the girl ter take it, the intercom sez, '5/2 Dawn Run.'

He goes ter sign the price on the slip.

—Forget the price, I shout.

—Can't, he sez, —if yer want it, yer got 9/4 or no bet.

The fuckin cunt, I'm thinkin, the fuckin bosses' man, where the fuck's God wid a spare cancer when yer need him.

—Yeah 9/4, I sez.

An I walk outside an go to consult me watch, which I aint got no more. There's a clock on St James's Church. I roll up the bettin slip an sez a prayer.

—Five till the off, I tell Debbie, an I notice she's cryin.

Not loud, *look at me* tears but silent *wot's gonna happen?* tears.

—Fuck kid, I sez, —this is a fuckin winner.

I look round the smoke-choked prefabricated ex-boy scouts hut that serves as Bosworth's Bookmakers. An it's true, every town is different but the inside of every bookies is the same. The same walls painted wid cigarette smoke an race cards, same stools, same short arse pens, the same hard luck stories, the same 'I was gonna back the winner but.....', the same hopeless smell a defeat.

An wot I'm really lookin at is me future.

I begin ter pick the paint on the grubby door.

The tannoy sez *they're goin down*. I get a sudden need for a shit.

—Wait here a second, I sez ter Debbie, as if she's got any fuckin choice.

I whip through the shop an down the side of the counter to the toilet. I'm just about through when I hear the commentator say, *They're under starters orders.... And they're off!*

I race outside leavin me jeans unzipped an me hands all smelly.

An we listen, stood next to a propped open bookies door, our whole future in the hands of a horse an man that we'll never meet. They come to three from home. Dawn Run an three others hit it tergether. I look over at Debbie. She's bitin her ringless fingers. They land over it, Run an Skip in front, but tirin. Wayward Lad in second, ours in third, an Forgive an Forget goin like a dream in fourth.

I've watched racin all me life. I know I'm beat. I crumple me ticket an throw it.

But then somethin weird an wonderful happens. The horse dint know its beat, an it battles back. O'Neill the crazy Irishman is throwin little Dawn Run at fences. An it's pluggin on relentlessly.

—Come on, God, just the fuckin once, yer miserable old cunt! I scream.

The four horses in a line look at Cheltenham Hill. Wayward Lad jumps in front, two from home, an goes away by two lengths. Dawn Run looks one paced an tired. They hit the last wid ours in third. I'm thinkin of the moonlight flit that me, Debbie an the kids gotta do. A hundred yards ter go an Wayward Lad's still two lengths up. But the Irish followers of Dawn Run start a roar, one of them roars that start up in a little field in County Clare an finishes up deafenin half of Gloucestershire. Dawn Run's ears prick an she gives it everythin. Ten yards from the post she catches Wayward Lad an passes it. The greatest show of guts an grace I've ever seen. *We've won, we've won, we've fuckin well won.* The bookies is in uproar, people I aint never seen cheerin for me. An me an Debbie are huggin each other an laffin an the babies are screamin. I pick up the sweat covered bettin slip an give it her, —It's all yours, I sez.

An we dance a jig of delight.

She stops mid spin, the whole bookies is starin at us.

—I love you, she whispers.

I'm stood outside the Lion an Lamb. The kids' taxi's late, but I got a smile on me face. Me an Debbie. That's it with love. Yer don't get ter choose who or how. An the one thing yer know about anyone yer love is that only one of four things can happen. You leave them, they leave you, you bury them or they bury you.

I'm stood outside that pub, waitin for me kids. As I'm toastin the mornin sky wid a hip flask that started life as a half of Gordons, the taxi pulls up. Out jump me four kids: Brendan, Rory, Eammon an Shannon, me own little Republican cell.

—Eight thirty, sez the taxi driver.

—Already? I sez, lookin at me watch as the kids snigger.

I hand him a tenner.

He drives off an I'm left wid me kids.

—Beryl sez yer a dickhead, Shannon sez.

—A fine judge of character your Auntie, I sez, — Why?

—Yer said Mr Asif wid the one arm was an Iraqi shoplifter, sez Brendan.

—Could be, I sez an laugh. —An anyway it was Asif who told me that joke, I add, an I realise the ex an her family are turnin me kids into the Hitler Youth. They even count the cans I drink. I pick up me bag a cans, say, —Six Stella an a hip flask is all I got ter declare. An we head for town.

The kids is bouncin along, how I want it. I want the day ter be fun an no cryin. I gotta keep the vibe up. I can't let this new man, this fuckin Gary, take me kids, he can't have em, their mine.

—Hey Shaz, I sez ter Shannon —how's school?

She shrinks back. —You're not comin there again are yer, dad?

An it breaks me fuckin heart. I give her little hand a squeeze an sez, —Just wonderin if you'd learnt anything new.

A light sparks in her eye. —Yeah, she sez, —Gary taught me how to make little cigarette packets from the top of an old one.......

Her words tail off, she knows that she's hurt me.

The kids can do anythin they like as long as they don't speak about their mother in a good light an especially they don't mention the new man's name.

—You okay, Dad? sez Brendan.

He's ten, the one I trust. He aint joined the enemy, yet.

—Yep, I sez.

We walk in silence a bit.

—It's just I wanted ter be the one ter teach yer things like that, I finally say.

As if I woulda, I think, all I ever did was get pissed.

—You don't even smoke normal cigs, Dad, sez Shannon.

An there goes her mother's favourite word, 'normal'.

We're outside Dillons the newsagents.

—Dad, sez little Eammon —can we have some toffees?

I peel off a twenty an sez, —Here, have a fiver each.

They trot in the shop happy ter fuck.

I'm pretendin ter read the adverts in the winda, but lookin beyond the bargains ter be had, at me kids. I'm like some distant Aunt or somethin, everytime I see em I think ter meself, *Oh haven't they grown.* That's me role now, any man she chooses ter live wid gets ter see em on a daily basis, while I'm not allowed near the door of me own house.

I watch little Shannon tryin ter pick a comic, her tiny face screwed up tryin ter choose. An I knock on the winda an sez, —get both! Who gives a fuck?

It reminds me of the bikes at Christmas. I wanted ter get them somethin that would blow any present she bought right out of the water so I took them to Halford's an spent nine hundred quid on the best four bikes they had. Now all four are in the garden shed wid punctures, not bin used in months. An every time a see them, they got new clothes on. Brendan an Rory have got on brand new United away shirts. Eammon, ever awkward, is a City fan, an he's got their new home shirt on. Shannon is wearin a pretty green dress from Next where her mam has an account. It's as if she's sayin that they don't need me no more, that me time has past. I note a graze on Shannon's knee. Who the fuck did that? I wonder, I'll ask about that. I mean yer can't be too careful can yer? Every time yer read about a kid assaulted it's a fuckin step-father. Fuckin step-father. Any of mine ever call this Gary person 'Dad' an I finish wid them for good.

Shannon comes out, she's spent up.

—Hold these, she sez an gives me a bag of assorted toffees an magazines.

—Who did that to yer leg? I ask.

—Fell off a bike, she sez.

—You tellin the truth? I ask in a concerned voice.

—Honest Dad, she sez, frightened.

I make a mental note ter ask Brendan about it if I get the chance. An believe me I'll make the fuckin chance.

—Got yer bike fixed then? I ask in a more cheery voice.

—Naw, she sez, —borrowed Laura's.

Before I can sez anythin I hear arguin from in the shop. It's gone off between Brendan an Rory.

—Wait here sweetheart, I sez ter Shannon an trot in.

Rory gettin shoved inter a magazine rack, knockin the Buntys an Batmans everywhere.

—Get yer toffees an stuff an stop messin about, I sez in a stern, Dad voice.

The young blonde girl comes from behind the counter an her an Eammon start ter pick the magazines up. I'm stood there wid me bag of drink. The girl's bent over wid her arse in the air, an me, Brendan an Rory are starin at her purple thong.

Rory notices me pervin an nudges Brendan an they start laffin, an it's infectious cos I start an can't stop. An poor old Eammon who's missin the view an aint got a clue wot he's laffin at, is gigglin loudest of all.

The poor girl finally gets the magazines back.

They pay for their stuff an we walk outside.

—Dad, why don't you call at our house no more? Brendan sez.

—Can't, son, I sez, —give us a bit of that Crunchie.

An I think about the night I got the injunction.

You could say it was all Nat King Cole's fault. He loved Nat King Cole me dad did, loved him ter fuckin bits, an he sang like him. We lived in a little prefab in Cheetham Hill then, an we were always skint. Me dad used ter shave in front of a mirra in the bathroom, an I'd be sat on the toilet watchin. It musta bin a Sunday cos me dad was a navvy, an in them days in the buildin game yer worked Saturday mornin. So it was a Sunday a million dreams ago, an he was lookin in a mirra, shavin wid a cut throat razor an singin, this amazin song, 'The dream had ended....'

I asked him one time did he make it up. An me dad said that he didn't, it was written by the greatest singer

61

of all time, but no one would ever recognise him as that cos he wore a different coloured coat from other people. That's how me dad described black people, wore different coloured coats, but deserved the same respect.

An wot the fuck has this got ter do wid anythin? She got a new man, the ex did. An she told me about him in a little kitchen in Newton Heath. An I don't care wot it sez on me death certificate, that's when I died. I never hit her, never left her short of money, an never went wid another woman. I just drank like me dad did.

An I went back ter fight for her that night. Me, silly fuckin pacifist, wanted ter fight. I rang up ter leave a message on the ansa-phone. I sez, —the first time he lays an hand on one of me boys, the first time he tries ter climb into bed wid me little girl, I don't just fuckin kill him, I fuckin kill you an all. Lettin some fuckin stranger sleep a piece of plasterboard away from me Angel.

An he picks it up, don't he?

—Come an fuckin try it, he sez.

I ring a taxi an go down.

It's a tortured journey. But I get there an I wanna fight like I never wanted ter fight before in me life. I wanna rip this fucker's head off. But he won't come out. She's screamin an beggin through the locked door.

—Please Duncan, don't. We just wanna be left alone.

I shout back, —Send me kids out an I'll leave yer alone forever.

An I don't know wot ter do, so I start kickin fuck out of the door an buttin it. She's in hysterics.

—GET THE FUCKIN POLICE, she's screamin.

I sorta retreat ter the other side of the road an look round. All the neighbours are out watchin. I put me

hand ter the side of me face an it's blood, snot an tears.
I look up an see me eldest at a bedroom winda, an
he's shoutin,

—DAAAAAAAAAARRRRRRRRRRDDDDDDDD

It's like a trumpet blast from Heaven. There's
rainbows in me heart an that's the point all the fightin
leaves me an I remember me dad an Nat King Cole
an bein hated for wot you are. Different coloured
coats. I'm stood wid a whole terrace street starin at
me, I hear a siren.

I look up at me first born, his face pressed against
the glass, an I start singin Nat King Cole to him. An
even though I'm gettin involved in armed robbery an
God fuckin knows wot, I'm feelin better. Okay, I still
cry, but not for as long as I used to. I swing Shannon's
arm an smile.

—Yer cryin Dad, sez Shannon.

—An eye infection, sez I, —an if there's any part of
the body prone ter infection then the ayes have it.

—Where we goin Dad? sez Shannon.

—Anywhere, sez I, hopin that me seven year old
can suggest somewhere that'll pull me out of the shit.

—Fun World? sez she.

—Fun World it is, sez I, —unless of course yer aint
got 20,000 Ugandan shillins. Then it aint fun.

—Are yer drunk, Dad? sez Shannon.

—No sweetheart, sez I.

We walk down the Avenue past where me dad got
killed by a hit an run an wait for a bus into town.

It's a good route is Rochdale Road, one every ten
minutes. We're stuck there waitin for half an hour,
the kids grow impatient. Rory's took ter vandalisin
the notice board. Normally I'd exercise parental
control, but if the fuckin bus company can't adhere to
a simple timetable then they deserve wot they get.

A pensioner stood nearby is shakin his head in

disgust.

—Say wot yer like about Thatcher, I shout even though he's only foot away, —but she had the buses runnin on time.

The pensioner looks away.

—Who's Thatcher? asks Brendan.

—Precisely Mr Nicely, I sez makin a mental note to ease up on the drink for an hour or two.

Shannon asks me to lift her on the shelter roof so she can see the bus as it leaves Alkrington, an in me drunken state it seems like a good idea. I'm just about to lift her up, much to the consternation of me fellow travellers, when Rory shouts, —Here it is!

An we all get on board.

The driver is Smiley Kennerly. Smiley grew up wid me in the maisonettes of Miles Plattin, so he just nods for me ter walk through wid the kids. Eammon is overawed: his dad can get him on buses for free.

The bus deposits its load outside Noble's Amusement Arcade, an I march us in.

Three foot inside the door we get stopped by a big, baldy fucker —Eighteen and over only, he sez.

—Don't be fooled by the grey hair, I sez, —I am.

—I'm sorry, he sez wid an unyieldin smile.

The day goes by. I just dole out money. We do McDonalds. We queue up for ten minutes an order our Big Macs. The mandatory spotty faced kid behind the counter sez, —Are you eating them here, sir?

To which I reply, —Don't be daft, luv, it'd hold the queue up.

The kids crack up. It's like the old days.

We head to Fun World. We walk through the door an it's loud an claustaphobic, wid kids runnin in every direction. Everyone not inflicted wid St Vitas' Dance is singin, *Happy birthday dear Dylan, happy birthday to you*. They let a few dozen balloons fall from a net suspended above.

—Dint know she was here? I sez ter Rory.

—Who? he asks.

—Annette, I sez.

—Annette who? he sez, fallin for it.

—A net wid balloons in it, I sez an start laffin.

I pay at the counter, they take off their shoes, an they're free ter run wild in wot is basically a kids' assault course, surrounded by pits of plastic balls. They run off screamin an shoutin. I buy a cup of orange an four Slushes an go an sit at a little plastic table wid a giant Father Christmas as company.

—This seat taken? I ask Santa.

Wid no answer forthcomin I claim the seat an start rootin through me bag for me gin. I'm just pourin it in the watery orange when Nadia stops me. I know she's called Nadia cos she's very helpfully got a name badge on.

—Can't do that, she whines, —no alcohol allowed. It's on the board as you come in.

—Who'll know? I sez an carry on pourin a liberal gin into the anaemic orange.

I look into her eyes an smile, but she's havin none of it. She looks round for help.

—Mr Harris! she shouts.

This bearded fucker comes over. He's wearin a sticker that sez Zak, an I immediately take a dislike ter Zak.

—Problem? he asks.

—No, I sez, —you?

—You're not allowed alcohol on these premises, he sez, —you either give the bottle to me or you leave.

There's maybe twelve adults sat around an they're all tuttin an doin concerned parent routines, bunch a miserable bastards.

—Seen enough? I sez indignantly, —Tut-tut-tut. It's

like a Skippy convention.

I stare at me audience an they look away.

The tanoy blares out, *It's Charlie the Clown time!*

I down the orange an give the gin bottle ter Harris.

—You're bein bing-bonged mate, I sneer.

He aint happy but then again neither am I.

—I'll expect it back untouched, I shout as he walks away.

I look up. Shannon is on a pirate walkway above. She's cryin. I've done it again, I've showed her up. She don't need ter go see Charlie, if she wants ter see a clown she looks at her dad.

I sit alone an friendless, apart from Santa.

We finish at Fun World an we head to Bury, spin around there a bit then jump on the tram for the journey back. This inspector gets on. I aint bought no tickets. Me kids look scared silly. Shannon squeezes me hand.

—Tickets please? sez he.

—Soz about this, sez I, sizzled, —but I bought returns in St Peter's Square an I've just took me children to Fun World an Rory there has left the tickets in a carrier bag on one of the tables.

—You always blame me, sez Rory an the kid could be an actor, —I gave it ter Brendan ter mind.

—No way, sez Brendan, —don't be puttin it on my toes.

An it's looks like it's gonna come ter blows.

The inspector moves on, he don't even fine me or demand the fare or nothin. I'm beginin ter think I'm indestructible.

We hit Manchester again. I take em on the Big Wheel in Piccadilly Gardens.

We're all sat in the same chair thing, Brendan an Rory together opposite me, Eammon an Shannon each side of me. It's snug, a proper family like. We've had a great day an I don't want it to end yet. The carriage jolts an we all shriek as the chains rattle an we're thrown against the restrainin bar. We're risin, leavin life far behind. An all the evenin stars are twinklin at us, reachin out through the smog an dirt of the skyline, an lightin our ascent. The kids are laffin an cheerin. An this is it, this is now, an a hundred solicitors wid a million clever words, can't take this away from me. When they're wid me they're mine, an I aint lost, I can't lose, not while these kids believe in me, I'm smilin an laffin an wavin an a thousand other things but beat. The wheel reaches its pinnacle, an comes to a halt.

The smell of the city is below us, an the taste of the petrol fumes is gone from our mouths. We can breathe, we can hear ourselves speak widout shoutin, we can feel the night air on our faces. The rat race an the rats can have the streets, we've soared above it all. Maybe it's fuckin temporary, but aint fuckin everythin?

Brendan whispers somethin ter Rory, an they giggle together, head touchin head, shoulder ter shoulder. The wind whips through our chair. Shannon cuddles up ter me an Eammon an Shannon grip me hands an we all rock tergether gently in the chair as the wind blows some more and the stars sparkle. An I wish it could stay this way forever. We're sat there rockin ter the creakin an crankin of the wheel. A restrainin bar an rusty chains holdin us in place.

—Look at that, yells Eammon —yer can see for yonks!

—It's true wot they say, I sez.

Wot? they ask in unison.

—That people seen from high up look just like ants.

—No they don't, sez Rory.

—Yeah they do, that one there looks just like your

Aunt Beryl.

An they laff. I don't think they understand the joke, they're laffin cos I'm laffin. It's the mood. We're swingin on stars. An it's all set out beneath me like a map of me life. The Cheetham skyline where I was born an raised, Oldham Street an the tower blocks that reach out into the sky like red-hatted giants an herald the entrance ter the Miles Plattin that I grew up in. Victoria station where I sold football pinks as a teenager. —FOOOOOTBALLLL PINK. GET YER PINK. ALL TERDAYS RESULTS. FOOOOOT BAWLLLLLLLLLLLLLLL PINK! The United floodlights in Old Trafford where I remember jibbin the turnstiles as a kid ter watch men who I thought were gods. The gasometers in Newton Heath, where me kids were born an where I had ter leave them when she got someone else. An the Blackley Hills ter the north, where I've finished up. An I look at the faces of me four kids. Smilin an in love wid life an wid me. These kids are mine, my blood, an no fuckers ever gonna take them away from me.

I take out me last can an cuddle Shannon to me chest. —I love you all, I sez, —don't never forget that. Tears are streamin down me face. I don't wanna send them home, I aint done nowt wrong, it aint fair.

An for the first time in the day a quiet as silent as a cockroach's fart falls over us.

The Big Wheel starts ter shiver, then begins its descent to Earth.

I look at me Newcastle Brown watch. I'm nearly an hour late in takin em home. I start singin 'The fog on the Tyne is all mine all mine' as the Wheel dips.

It's past goin home time. Shannon's cryin. Brendan sez, —Dad we gotta go home or me mam won't let us come no more.

I flag down a taxi, an they all kiss me an get in it.

I watch it zoom away. Shannon's wavin right until the taxi moves out of me sight.

A One Socked Man

All of a sudden it's Friday mornin an I'm lyin in bed wid me dick in me hand, wonderin whether ter get up or get it up, when the buzzer goes.

—Buzz, buzz-buzz, buzz-buzz-buzz.

It's the code, so I throw some clothes on an go ter answer it. It's Steve.

—Wot yer want? I sez, lookin furtively about. I drag him in.

—Yer not supposed ter come here. Why aint yer got gloves on?

—It's fuckin warm, he sez.

—Right, I sez, —don't touch nowt.

I run into the kitchen an get two plastic Aldi bags an I make him put em on his hands.

—Fuckin para you, he sez an sits down, starin at his Aldi gloves.

—I told yer not ter come here, I sez.

—Karen's havin an affair, he sez.

—Munffle-fluffen-dolph, I sez in shock an fear.

—I know, he sez, —but I can't figure out who. You any ideas?

—Me? I sez, —you're imaginin it. Ease up buddy.

—No, he continues, —it could be the fuckin winda cleana. I seen her gettin inter his van.

This stops me in me tracks. He thinks it's Maurice.

—Yeah, yer could be right, I sez, —I've heard whispers about him meself.

—Wot should a do? he sez, scannin me face for enlightenment.

—Calm down, in three days yer got a quarter of a mill, wot's Mr Fuckin Woo got? I sez.

—Mr Woo was a laundry man, not a winda cleana, he sez.

An I get the gin out.

We're sat there wordless an slurpin. All of a sudden he takes off his Aldi bags an gets a little wrap of brown out. *Aw ter fuck*, I think, *this I don't fuckin need.*

—Want the short straw? he enquires.

—Naw, I sez, —gin's enough for me.

—It'll clear yer sinuses, he sez. But I decline.

I watch him heighten his senses.

—She's bin actin different, he sez.

—In wot way? I sez, hopin that I aint in anyway incriminated.

—Fuckin baffin all the time, he sez, —she never used ter bother much.

—Fuckin hell Steve, I sez, —she takes an interest in a bar of soap an yer wanna kill her?

An he sees the funny side of it.

—If she goes anywhere near the toothpaste, then I'll do her, he laughs.

An I think I've got him a bit settled. We sit an discuss the plan. He's got to know it inside out in all his altered states of mind, I've decided.

—I ring you, I sez, —second I leave the casino. You head for Chadderton, an get in the house. She comes home. You let her get in an then yer gotta get her calm an tie her up. The kid comes home the next mornin, the door's open. Yer get the kid calm, an yer tie her up. You an Bella go ter the casino in her car. I'm outside waitin for her ter unlock as per normal. You instruct Bella ter instruct me, 'fire check, leave the cameras off'. I go behind the Reception counter. There'll be two croupiers, a cashier an a valet maid there. They'll go for a brew an ter change into their uniforms. You an Bella load up the case an leave. She instructs me ter tell the Pit boss that she'll be back in about forty five minutes. An you an Bella go ter Broadhust playin fields. You explain that she's bein watched from a tower block opposite an that if she

71

moves then you'll ring yer accomplice an the kid gets it. Karen in the meantime will have locked the tied up sprog in the cubby-hole, got in your car which will be parked near the Railway, an headed off ter meet you behind the Gardeners Arms. You'll leave Bella's car on Moston Lane East, an walk ter the Gardeners. You then count an split the cash three ways, an remember I'll know exactly wot was in that bag. You give Billy my share an two grand for him. Then we don't get in touch again ever.

We go through it several times an he gets it every step. He stays about an hour an then I spend about an hour cleanin up. I'm obsessed that the police'll finger print me flat.

I'm in work Friday night wid Colin when they post the next week's rota. As normal it's me an Smithy on the Saturday night an I do the Sunday dinner on me own. It's one of them easy Friday nights, wid not many ID's ter do. Everythin's goin same as usual. About three in the mornin who should come in but an ex-Soap actor an his latest conquest. It's a girl I grew up with, Lorraine Burns, though she calls herself Tiffany Derbyshire now. We shared a catechism together as kids, had some good times. I look Lorraine in the face all those dreams later an sez, —Can I take your coat, Tiffany?

She lets me take it without a hint of recognition, then swans inter the casino on the ex Soap actor's arm an don't look back.

The night goes by without any further incident. It gets ter four an we're kickin em out. Kerry the valet maid sez, —You goin ter the Press Club?

I count me tips. Twenty three quid: nineteen in cash an four in chips, an think, fuck it, enough for a few cans a Stella an a taxi home.

—Yeah, I sez, —how many goin?

—The usual. About six or seven, she sez.

It's weird. In casinos there's a sort of caste system. Reception, kitchen an the bar staff all stick tergether, an the croupiers, bunch a prima donnas, stick to their own.

Let me tell you somethin, if you read the *Evenin News* you'll be lured into believin all this 24 hour City nonsense. As fuckin if. If your a late night worker in the Metropolis of Manchester, four o'clock gives you two options, one, the Press club, an two, Mamma's Kitchen on the market. So each mornin at about four, bouncers, cab drivers, casino workers an sundry subterraneans meet up in one or the other. Tonight we aim for the Press. It's me, Kerry, Colin, Meesha, Chad, Roy the Chef an Harvey the Doorman.

At the Press it's two-fifty a can of Stella, so we don't drink in rounds. I get meself four in an sit in the corner. The others arrive at the table. The night soon gets goin. Roy the chef an Meesha are arguin about the best way to make a goat curry.

—I'm a chef, yells Roy in a theatrical voice, —I ought ter know.

—An I'm a Jamaican, laffs Meesh, —so I know better.

I interrupt their banter.

—You know Robinson Crusoe? I ask.

—Waaaaa? snarls Roy.

—The book about the man that got marooned, I sez, —it was real, he existed.

They all stare at me.

—Wot's that got to do with the best way to cook goat? asks Roy.

—The book was based on a man called Alexander Selkirk.

—And? sez Roy.

—Well, all there was ter eat on the island was rats or goats, an he dint fancy rat, so he ate goat. An he used ter shag em as well.

—Yer fuckin jokin, sez Colin.

—Bollocks, sez Harvey.

—True, I sez, —after forty year they turn up an they find him, an he admitted it.

They're all lookin at me like I'm a Rampton case.

—Some goats he ate, I add, —an some goats he shagged. But he never ate any that he shagged.

—Rass, tuts Meesha, —I'll never be able to eat goat again without a vision of a man humpin one comin into my head.

Chad's rockin wid laughter, he's a shy Asian kid.

For some reason the conversation moves onto music.

Kerry asks me, —Can you play any musical instrument, Drunk?

—Naw, I sez, —bought that *Play the Guitar in Five Minutes* thing by Bert Weedon. I think he musta bin on weed. I gave it three-quarters of an hour an still couldn't figure out how ter play it. Guess I'm just a slow learner.

—I was in an orchestra at school, sez Chad.

—Playin wot? asks Kerry.

—The triangle, sez Chad, bein perfectly serious.

I nearly choke on me pint. Harvey lets out a guffaw that has heads turnin.

—Honest, sez Chad.

 I'm rockin in me chair.

—The fuckin triangle, laughs Colin, —how hard is that?

—Hey, yells Roy, —you could replace him with a microwave, just set it ter ping at the right time.

Harvey gets the beer in while we have some fun

with Chad.

—Ever get asked ter join the Stones? sez someone.

—Yeah, the Wildman of the triangle, giggles Kerry.

—Did yer double up on tambourine? I ask.

—Ever get asked to tour wid U2 an do a triangle solo? shouts some fuckin interested stranger on the next table.

It's hard ter tell wid Chad's complexion, but I bet he's hot with embarrasment.

It's all died down by the time Harvey comes back from the bar. He puts the drinks down then not only goes over to the pool table an gets the triangle that they use to rack the balls. He comes back carryin that an a pen, taps Chad on the shoulder an sez, —Go on, see if yer can get a tune outta that.

The table's in hysterics.

—Let's hear the March of the Valkyrie in D Minor, I shout above the din.

Chad's game, I got to give him that. He has a go.

An the beer flows, an flows an flows.

I wake the next afternoon about half twelve. It's Chinese Moon Cake Day. The day we turn over the casino. I'm shakin as I shave. The phone goes. I clean off the soap an answer it. It's me mate, Macca. I aint seen much of him of late due ter the burden of work an the bigger burden of shaggin Kaz.

—Right Drunk? he sez.

—Yeah. You? I sez.

—Not bad, he sez.

Silence.

—You out terday? he sez.

—Naw, work ternight, I reply.

Silence.

—United doin well, I sez.

—Yeah, he sez.

—Bin goin? I sez.

—Yeah, he sez, —with Benny an Rigga.

Silence.

—Right then, I sez.

—Yeah, he sez.

An I'm just about ter say *see ya* an hang up, when he whips the carpet from under me.

—Hey, hear about Maurice the winda cleana? he sez.

Right away me mind shoots ter Strange Steve.

—Wot? I sez.

—Murdered, he sez.

—Wot? I sez, —yer jokin?

—No. Back a the Clary.

—Who'd wanna shoot him? I sez.

—Wot yer on about, shoot? he sez, —he got battered ter death. Shoot? Where you fuckin livin?

—Right, I sez, —did they get whoever done it?

—How the fuck should I know? he sez.

—Aw this is fuckin terrible, I sez, —yer've knocked the fuckin stuffin outta me.

An I sit down by the side of the phone an me minds goin *hurdy-gurdy* but can I fuck think wot ter do next.

—Dint know yer liked him, Drunk, sez Macca.

—Yeah, he was sorted, I sez.

—But he showed yer up in the Robin Hood, Macca sez, —made a cunt out of yer cos you were four week behind wid the windas.

—Yeah but that's no fuckin reason ter murder him, is it? I sez.

—Fuck, you're takin this hard, he sez. —You goin or wot?

—Goin where? I sez.

—Maurice's funeral, he sez.

76

—No way, I sez, —he was nowt ter me.

An I know I gotta break the rules an get a hold of Strange Steve before the position becomes irretrievable.

—Right Macca, I sez, —I'll see yer.

—Yep Drunk, he sez, —yer a weird fucker. An he hangs up.

I'm sat on the floor, the phone to me ear. I dial Steve's mobile.

His ansa phone comes on:

—You're through ter Steve, whip cracker woo.....whip cracker woo.....whip cracker way.....please leave yer message at the tone.

—Steve, it's Drunk, you there? I sez.

He picks it up.

—Drunk are yer daft? Yer said no contact, he sez in a jolly voice.

—Maurice is dead, I sez.

—It's the talk a Monsall, he sez, —bludgeoned ter death outside the Clary.

—Was it you? I ask haltingly.

—Me who wot? he laughs, —put the rhyme in the rhyme a lime a ding dong?

—Steeeee, I start a say.

But he interrupts an sez, —Yer told me to, Drunk.

I'm shakin. —DID I FUCK, I yell —I SAID, 'LEAVE IT'.

—You said he had a reputation.

—I fuckin said? I sez, —I never said batter the fuck out of him with a.......... Wot did yer use?

—A snooker ball in a football sock, he sez, —crashed his skull like Humpty-Dumpty. Blood, snot an wot little brains he had everywhere.

I throw up. No warnin or no nothin. I just puke on the phone. —Uuggggggleee-uph, I'm goin down the phone.

—You blowin raspberries at me yer little twat? he

sez.

—I'm bein sick, I sez.

—Bin on the piss? he enquires.

—Look, I whine, —let's call the casino job off till things settle down.

—NO, he sez firmly, —we go ahead.

I'm too ill ter argue.

—Don't worry, he sez, —they got no reason ter suspect me.

Then in a complete change of conversation, he starts ter tell me about the Birkenhead Principle:

—Yer know wot it is? he asks.

—No, I sez, thinkin it may have some bearin on reality.

—On a ship, he continues, —if it's sinkin they have wot they call the Birkenhead Principle. It means women an children first. But we're all supposed ter be equal, aint we? So why not just the kids first? I bet there weren't any women on the Titanic wonderin round shoutin, 'I demand equality....... I wanna drown!'

He's laffin. He murdered a man last night an he's laffin. *Aw ter fuck an back*, I think. —See yer, I sez.

An things start not ter feel so good.

I check me watch. It's one fifteen. I don't start work till eight thirty, so there's time ter kill an I gotta stay soberish. I take a clean white shirt, put that an me casino trousers in a bin bag an head for me mam's. I get ter the octogenarians for half past, an give the door a good clatterin on account of her failin hearin. She answers about five minutes later.

—Okay, she sez, —yer don't have ter knock like a rentman. I aint deaf.

—Lend us twenty? I sez.

—Sorry, she sez carryin on the joke, —I'm as deaf as a post in that ear. Wot do yer want? she asks.

—Nowt. Will yer iron me casino gear? I ask.

An we sit down.

Me mind's leapin all over the fuckin shop. Murder. An fuckin pointless murder at that. Wot the fuck have I got meself involved in? A couple a month from now an I could be sharin a cell wid Big Nobby, who dint earn the non de plume Big Nobby cos of his height. I nip to the toilet. There's a feelin in the pit of me stomach of raw fear. I wash the stale sweat from me face an silently tell the mirror that I wish me dad was still alive ter tell me wot the fuck ter do. I open the medicine cabinet door. Me mam's sleepers are sittin there. She got em after me dad died, but the stubborn bugger's never took a one. I take two out of the bottle, put em in a bit of toilet tissue, an stick em in me back pocket then fuck off downstairs.

I look at me mam's agein face. She could be a poker player, it gives nowt away. More lines than the Moon or Greater Manchester trams put tergether. Lived in the same city all her life. This woman actually remembers the Germans bombin Manchester, sat all night on a staircase nursin her younger brother as Wallworks went up in smoke an the Irish family two doors away got killed when a bomb landed directly on top of their house. Life aint bin kind ter her, married an aimless drunk, an got an aimless drunk for a son. Worked doin three jobs at once when we were kids an me dad was laid off. She only had two holidays in thirty year. I know she holds it against me that me marriage failed, an I couldn't hold on ter me kids, which meant she lost her grankids by proxy. I know I've always let her down. I look at the grey hair an think, *How many of them fuckers did I put there?* The casino robbery is me only hope, the last pistol shot of a dyin gunman.

—Want a brew? I ask.

—Put the water in an I'll brew it, she sez, —I want a proper cup.

I smile ter meself an think about when the local shopkeeper put up a sign sayin that the kids from the local school were not allowed in his shop because of the continued shopliftin. No problem there yer might think, his shop, his business. But the local school is a Catholic school an me mam's got a long memory an seen all this *No Catholic Here* business before. An in her eighty-second year she takes up the fight. But there's a twist. The local shopkeeper, Mr Patel, doesn't know a Catholic school from a Protestant school, an wots more he couldn't care. But she tells him that her an hers an any other right minded person wouldn't shop there again. Old Patel, he's got pride, an he refuses ter take the sign down. So I can't use Patel's cos he's anti-Catholic. But we still let on an he always asks how me mam is. Strange things, principles.

—Do yer know, she sez, —that this Pope has created more saints than all the other Pontiffs put tergether?

—Well that's good int it? I sez.

—But we're livin in ungodly times, she sez.

—Yeah but it might be like the GCSE's, I sez, —if yer average in a bad year you're a genius.

She smiles. She likes a good theosophical debate.

—They'll be sellin Papal Clemencies next, she sez.

We sit an drink the brew. Me mam's not accumulated a lot in her eighty year of honesty. A set of religious figures on the fireplace, nine in all, plus a wooden carvin of The Last Supper, (whoever organised that piss up deserved crucifyin). I notice the St Joseph's Penny Box on the windasill, an sling a fiver in it.

—Feelin generous aren't you? she sez an smiles.

I shrug. I can't settle, I need a proper drink.

—Right mam, I sez, —gotta get goin.

I get up ter leave. As I get ter the lobby door, I look back.

—Don't forget ter iron me uniform.... An thanks mam, I sez.

—Wot for? she sez.

—Just about everythin, I sez, an exit.

I'm dyin for two things: a good drink an a good shag. I ring Kazzer's mobile in the hope of killin two sparrers wid one ducker.

She picks it up right away. Too fuckin right away for me.

—Yeah? she sez.

—Can yer speak? I sez.

—Better than Helen Keller, she replies, laffin.

—Well this'll bring yer back down ter Earth, I sez, —Maurice the winda cleana will be missin no more corners, he's dead.

—Yeah, I know, she sez.

—Yeah but wot yer don't know is.......STEVIE BOY KILLED HIM.

—Yeah I know, she sez.

An I'm lost.

—Yer know? I sez.

—Yeah, she sez, —I was with him.

—WHY? I wail.

—Steve found out he was shaggin me, she sez, gigglin.

—How? I ask.

—I told him, she sez.

—Jeez us fuckin Christ, I sez. —Why? He was a decent bloke.

—Yer weren't sayin that when he showed yer up over owin him four weeks money.

—No, but I dint want him dead.

—Yer shoulda seen it, Drunk, she sez, —blood everywhe........

—Enough, I sez, —I already got a mental picture in me head.

—We did it for you, Drunk, she sez.

—Yer wot? I squeal.

An I might be gettin a little bit paranoid, but I swear I can hear Steve laffin in the background.

I hang up.

I head for Macca's flat in the rain-kissed skies of Miles Plattin, stoppin as I go for the mandatory carryout of vodka an Stella. I get there an give him the tribal buzz. He opens, an he's genuinely glad ter see me.

—Thought you had work? he sez.

—Not till half eight, I sez, walkin into the kitchen for two glasses.

—Wot you bin up ter? he sez.

—Fuck all, I sez defensively.

He's bin me mate a lotta years has Macca, we married an divorced two sisters, so we've a lot in common.

—Anythin ter go wid the vodka? I ask.

—Diet coke under the sink, he sez.

I pop me head down an look under the sink.

He's got a drippin waste an it's leakin onto a litre of shite coke.

—Twenty nine pence a bottle? I shout.

—Yeah they were out of the cheap stuff, he shouts back.

I wander inter the livin room carryin the glasses.

Me mind goes back ter his divorce. Me an Macca got there early an we book in wid the usher. We tell him we'll be havin a smoke in the outter waitin room if we're needed. We're sat there mindin our own buisness. Twenty minutes later the usher come out an sez ter Macca, —Mr McLeash, they're calling you.

An Macca quick as a flash, sez,

—Well if they're callin me they're leavin someone else alone.

An that's wot I like about him, he can always make me smile. I'm tempted to tell him about tonight's plan but I'd only be makin him an accessory.

—Funny business about Maurice Windas, he sez.

—Probably drugs, I sez, —usually fuckin is.

—Naw, not the sort, he sez.

—Then how do I know? I sez, —it could be the outbreak of the Monsall Shammy Leather Wars.

—Still a fuckin wife an four left behind, he sez, —a bit naughty.

—Fuckin hell Macca, I sez, —I come here for a quiet drink not ter hear about some winda cleana.

An I pull out a spliff.

—Here, I sez, —wot's happenin between you an Serenity?

The last time I was down they'd bin arguin an she'd fucked off back to her mother's.

—Sorted, he sez, smilin. —Yer remember when I said to yer that seein yer ex wife wid another man was like seein Denis Law in a City shirt?

—No, I sez, tryin ter see some sorta connection.

—Yeah, yer wanna hate em but yer can't cos of all that's gone before. An the losin of the kids that was like Denis's back heel against United. That's wot sent me down. Relegated ter the Nationwide Depression League.

I'm nonplussed. Wot the fucks he on about? I thought he was through all that mopin shite.

—But, he adds, —time goes by an along comes Eric Cantona. An Serenity's me Cantona. She's done for

83

me wot Eric did for United.

—If yer could paint that thought yer could put it on a chocolate box, I sez, swillin back me vodka.

I look at me watch. It's 2.30.

—Hey, guess who I seen at Albert Bridge House when I was havin me medical? he sez.

—Doctor Singh? I sez.

—Darren Boreland, he sez.

—That was gonna be me second guess. Who the fuck is he?

—Remember Irish Daley? he sez.

An I do. When me an Macca were teenagers we were in the same class at school as Irish Daley an Darren Boreland. Borland was the cleverest, best lookin, most charmin an most revered kid in the school. An as if God hadn't given him enough aces ter play wid, he was also the best footballer, cricketer an fighter as well. All the girls loved him, but none loved him as much as he loved himself.

Irish Daley meanwhile was some ordinary kid who was called Irish Daley cos there was an English Daley in our class. Irish was quiet an about as interestin as a runny boil. He couldn't stand football, he couldn't understand cricket an he didn't fight. Then one day his mother goes cleanin for a neighbour, a widower, an the inevitable happens, she takes off wid him. The neighbour makes a stipulation, he'll have her but not the kids. Mrs Daley bein the woman that she was, accepts the deal. So Irish Daley is left at home wid his dad. His clothes stop gettin washed, he looks unkempt, an he falls asleep in class. So now he's the butt of all our humour, an he takes it. That's until one day on the stairs, Irish is walkin up an stood in front of him are Boreland plus two girls from the year above. Boreland wants ter impress the girls so he starts singin the chirpy cheap song, the one that goes, 'I woke up this mornin an me mammy was gone'. An it had ter be noted that he had a good singin voice ter go wid everythin else.

We all fall about laffin. Not only is he the strongest an wisest but the God damn funniest as well. An there it woulda ended but Boreland buoyed by the success of his song said, —Daley, yer mam's a whore.

Daley can't raise his head, he's too ashamed. He starts cryin.

—Me mammy's no whore, he mumbles.

There they were perched on them stairs, the Goliath of Borland an the David of Daley. An Daley plunged at Boreland wid the rage an madness of righteousness. It was the biggest batterin I'd ever seen, an when it was over poor little Daley lay in a pool of his own blood. When he got up after Borland had fucked off, he did it wid a dignity that I have never forgot.

But it didn't end there. Three days later in Technical Drawin Daley tried ter stab Boreland wid a compass an took another almighty tatterin.

This went on for week after week. Every time Daley seen Borland he screamed, *Me mammy aint no whore*, an attacked him. Until they finally excluded Daley.

But in the weeks in between a strange thing had happened. Boreland lost his invincibility. He didn't seem unbeatable anymore. He'd bin offered out by one kid an he'd declined. An others like meself had taken ter answerin him back. Then one day he gets a knee injury an no more football career. An then spots. The worst case of acne I'd ever seen, an the girls don't find him irresistible anymore. An I'm stood smokin one day starin at him, wantin ter impress a girl, just like he did on the stairs wid Daley. So I'm starin him out.

—Wot you starin at? he sez, —I aint got two fuckin

heads.

—Some of yer spots have, I sez, puttin me arm round the girl as everybody laughs.

An that was it with Boreland. After that he just faded away. Until now.

—Wot's he up to? I ask.

—Works at the sick place, he sez.

—Wot, as a doctor? I sez.

—No, he hands out the numbers when yer go in, sez Macca, —gone fuckin bald too.

We piss our sides laffin.

An Macca sez, —Imagine, one day Daley's gonna walk through the Albert Bridge House door an scream *Me mammy's no whore*, an Borland has ter start all over again.

An I aint no believer or nothin but I like ter think that God was on them stairs that day, an when Boreland called Daley's mam a whore, God thought, *Yer not on, son, from now on yer on yer own.*

We sit there havin the crack, an time flies by. I fall asleep, an wake at six-thirty.

—Macca, wake up! I'm shoutin, —I'm late for work!

—Wot? he sez, —wot the fuck can I do about it?

—Ring us a taxi, I sez, gettin me things tergether.

He jumps up an rings Fran. Co Taxis.

As he does so he notices the time:

—Fuck me, yer got two hours yet, he sez.

—No Macca, I sez all panicky, —I gotta be early.

—Two fuckin hours, he sez, then alters his voice as the taxi firm answer his call —yes taxi please...... blah blah blah....

I pour meself a quick vodka an Weight Watchers.

He puts the phone down an sez, —Twenty minutes.

—Fuckin hell, I sez, —I'm in a hurry.

—Calm down, he sez, —yer gonna have a heart attack.

I start ter pace up an down.

—You shaggin that Crazy Karen or wot? he sez, takin me aback.

—Am I fuck, I lie.

He shrugs an pours himself the last of the vodka.

—Remember when we robbed White's telly shop? he sez.

An I smile.

—Me an you, aged about twelve, jibbed the door, he sez.

—Yeah, I sez.

—An we rummaged downstairs an got the petty cash, he carries on, —an we snook upstairs an opens a door.

I'm laffin.

—An the manager was fuckin the girl off the till on a little mattress, he laughs, —an I turn ter run but I run inter you, an yer mesmerised just starin at her.

—First pair a tits I'd ever seen, I sez.

—Yeah, an yer behavin the same now about Karen's tits, he sez. —Turn an run yer silly fucker. He pulls on his Super Kings dimp an adds, —I was in YP wid that Steve an it aint no fuckin act, he's certifiable. He used ter torture cockroaches. Watch yer fuckin back.

Before I can hardly take in wot he's sayin I hear the taxi beep.

I jump inter the beat-up old taxi. The driver is Max.

—Right Max? I sez, —the casino please.

—You okay, Drunk? he asks.

—Yep, I sez.

An he drives me there. There's a sign in the taxi sayin, Do Not Consume Food Or Drink In The Taxi,

87

an I wouldn't need tellin twice, the fuckin thing aint hygienic enough for me ter consider eatin in it. Max takes a fast right an splutters phlegm all over me.

—Could do wid a valet this could, I sez.

—Do it then, sez Max dimpin a cig out, —not mine, it belongs ter Franco.

We reach the casino an it's a fiver. I go ter pay him an it dawns on me. —Aw fuck, I sez, —me uniform. Max run me ter Blackley will yer? I look at me watch. It's ten past seven.

We head back up Rochdale Road towards Blackley, listenin ter Jazz FM.

He gets me to me mam's. I give the door the usual hammerin but ter no avail. So I head round the back an get the key from where it's hid an get in. I find the casino uniform slung over a chair, an a note on the coffee table:

—Duncan,
Ironed uniform. Left some dinner in microwave.
Back at eight. Lock up after yourself.
   Mam.

I aint got time for food so I undress an redress in a hurry. I bung me dirty clothes in the linen basket an I check me money. I've still got sixty quid of the two ton I drew out last week left. That's one of the bonuses of workin in a casino, yer can live on yer tips if necessary.

I rush out ter the taxi.

—Right Max, I sez, —the casino.

Off we go, right into heavy traffic. We get ter the corner of Victoria Avenue an Rochdale Road. There's bin an accident so we carry on over ter the Avenue East an head on down ter Hollinwood Avenue. Mistake. As we get near Warbeck the traffic's gridlocked. I'm sat bitin me nails. I notice this piece of graffitti on the side of Moston train station. In four feet high letters someone has written WHATEVER. An I'm thinkin, that's just how I feel, there's nothin God can throw at me now that'll make me give a flyin fuck about anythin. Max changes the radio channel an we catch the last bit of an interview wid Debbie Fallon, the grief stricken wife of the murdered winda cleana Maurice.

—.....He was a lovely man, lived for his kids. He wouldn't harm a soul. An............ (she breaks down sobbin).......... just pray that whoever's done this rots in Hell.

Maurice's ex-partner Denis Moore goes on ter add —*No man had a better mate.*

The report then confirms that Police have found what they believe to be the murder weapon. It don't reveal what, but I've an idea that Collyhurst CID are lookin for a one socked man who likes the odd game of snooker.

We finally edge down Warbeck an hit Broadway, which takes us onto Oldham Road, an there we get a bit a luck wid the traffic. Max drops me outside the casino for a second time.

—How much, hombre? I ask.

—Just give us a tenner an buy us a pint next time I see yer, he sez.

I bung him a tenner.

I walk down the casino stairs. I gotta look normal cos everythin's on camera. Colin is behind the counter finishin his day shift.

—Right, Col? I sez.

—Yeah, it's fuckin hammered, he sez.

I walk behind the counter an go ter the mirra. I

put me dicky-bow on, pat down me hair an sing, 'I'm just too good to be true'.

—Yer need a coffee, Drunk, Colin sez.

—I'll do the check, I sez, —then you can fuck off.

The check consists of checkin all the fire doors, an makin sure access isn't obstructed in case of fire. I don't really check fuck all, I just amble round lettin on ter people. Then I go down the stairs ter the kitchen an valet. Kerry's there an Carol. Roy the chef walks in from the restaurant.

—Goin to the Press tonight, Drunk? Roy sez.

—Yeah probably, I sez. I gotta keep things real I think, an I never refuse an offer that revolves round a drink.

—Got a bowl a soup I can have? I ask.

I'm feelin shit, but I know I have ter eat.

—Ian'll do you one in a minute, he sez, pullin out the *Evening News* crossword.

The crossword is a kinda ritual wid Roy. He passes every shift tryin ter complete it.

—Right, he sez, —what are you like on Literature?

—I know a bit, I sez.

—'Not wavin but drownin', who wrote it? he asks. Me blood runs cold. *Why that poem on this day?*

—Well? he sez, —a bowl a soup rests on it.

—Stevie Smith, I sez.

—Sure? he asks.

—Yeah, I sez, an he fills in the blanks, folds up the crossword an puts it away.

I have me soup (chicken an sweet corn) an fuck off back upstairs. I have ter sign the register in the Manager's office. As I get there the door's ajar. I can see Bella talkin ter Sancho the Pit boss. I knock.

—Lo, I sez, —chocker ternight.

—Are we sober? asks Bella.

I smile an sign in.

—Who are you on with tonight, Duncan? she asks.

—Smithy, I sez.

—Laurel and Hardy no less, she sez.

I smile again an she turns her attention ter Sancho.

—Watch Matthew Lees, he looks rather stoned, I hear her say.

I head back towards Reception pickin up a black coffee as I go. When I get there Smithy's arrived an she's chattin ter Colin.

—Kung Hey Fat Choy, she sez.

—Yer wot? I sez

—Kung Hey Fat Choy, she repeats.

—It's Moon Cake Day, I sez, —not fuckin New Year. That was February.

—What's it matter? she sez, laffin.

—Well yer wouldn't wish someone Merry Christmas on Saint Valentine's Day would yer? I sez.

I'll ter yer somethin about Smithy, first time I seen her I didn't like her. I dreaded workin a shift wid her. She's early twenties an inter fashion an wot have yer. I thought give it a week an she'll be readin me stars out an wantin ter do a make-over on me. But we got on like a house party on fire from the beginnin.

Colin counts his tips. Nineteen quid, not bad for a dinner.

—Should do well tonight, he sez.

I go behind to survey the coats taken. There's about twenty mooncakes there.

—Whose are the cakes? I shout.

—LC. Ho 676, he shouts back. —Want one?

It's a piss take.

Colin's taxi arrives an he fucks off up the stairs, forty ter the dozen. His night's planned, a bottle of Jack Daniels an the football on the telly.

Me an Smithy settle down for a long shift, me starin inter space an Smithy studyin her Highway Code.

—Wot's the stoppin distance for a lorry doin forty mile an hour? I ask.

She shrugs.

—The length of a pub car park, I sez.

I end up testin her on the Highway Code. Which passes half an hour an confirms me opinion that she'll never pass the test.

—Yer've no chance, I sez, —yer can't get one right.

—I'm okay at the drivin part, she sez seriously, — what's it matter if I don't know a few of the signs and signals?

Me mind's wonderin. I could pull the plug on the plan. At this point I've done nothin wrong. Well, apart from conspiracy ter rob, an accessory after the fact ter murder. Which if yer think about it is a pretty shitty charge. I mean big deal I knew about it after it happened. So does anybody who reads a paper. All I'm guilty of is mindin me own business. I'm shaken out of me restructure of the criminal justice system by the immediate presence of The Hat. When it comes ter the Chinese I've met thousands, an I can honestly say I've liked many more than I've disliked. But I fuckin hate Hat. He's ignorant an aggressive.

—Chee Sing, he sez ter me, barin a mouth full of green teeth wid gold fillins.

—A couple a white ones an yer'd have the Tricolour, I sez, ignorin his insult.

He takes a two pence out of his pocket, an places it on his hand.

—Take, he sez, laffin.

—No, Hat, I sez smilin, —your grip too strong.

—Ha, he laughs, an sez somethin in Cantonese that I don't understand.

He flings the twopence in the tip jar.

—Cheers, Hat, I sez, —the kids can eat again now.

Smithy laughs. An that's when it gets naughty.

Normally I couldn't give a fuck about Hat but he sez somethin ter me that strikes a chord in me heart.

—Mate-say-bet, he sez pushin his smelly fuckin face inter mine.

I move back.

—Mate-say-bet (your Mother's a whore), he repeats.

An I remember the little Irish kid called Daley. How against all odds he stood up an wouldn't stop standin up.

—Do-lay-lo-mo-lie (you no good fuckin bastard), I answer back.

—WHHHHAAAAAA! he wails. Harvey leaves his door duties an comes trottin down the stairs.

Now Harvey don't like Hat, an Hat don't like Harvey.

—What's up? sez Harvey.

Hat points at me an sez, —Mate-say-bet.

—Hear that? sez Harvey gently pushin The Hat towards the door, —His mate's a vet.

Hat goes upstairs mutterin an swearin in Cantonese as the internal phone rings.

—It'll be an ID, sez Smithy, an picks it up.

—It's for you, Smithy tells me.

I take the phone off Smithy.

—Office, forthwith, sez Bella, on the phone I'm holdin.

—Goin a see Bella, I sez puttin the phone down.

—Remember the Tolpuddle Martyrs, sez Harvey.

I walk through the crowded casino an I'm half hopin I get sent home. I could just pack up an head for me brother's in Cambridge.

I get ter the door, knock an enter.

Bella is chewin a toffee. —What on earth is happening? she sez.

—In wot way? I ask.

—Don't mess with me, you're clearly drunk, she

sez, —I can send you home for that.

It's strange but even though I'd never pass no breathalyser this is the soberest I've bin for a good while.

—Look Duncan, she sez, —I've been divorced as well and I understand it isn't easy. I feel for you with the kids. But can you blame your wife? You're drunk stupid each and every time she lets you have them. You need time to sober up. And get your muddled head firmly back in the real world.

I'm taken aback, this woman is actually showin some compassion.

—Now I'm going to do you a favour, she continues, —we don't want to lose you. But you absolutely cannot insult The Hat. Have you any idea how much we lose when the Chinese do a walk out?

—A lot, I sez timidly.

An the casino does. If the Chinese don't like a change in the rules or don't get some concession, they walk out. Just down the Marjong an leave en masse ter Soames Casino or somewhere else. They hold the casino ter ransom. No Chinese person will cross the casino step while the dispute is on.

—Exactly, Bella sez, —your last shift is tomorrow. The day after that I want you to take a week's holiday. Come back when you've got yourself all straightened out. You need a rest.

Why couldn't she have done this last week?

—Finish tomorrow and return, smart, sober and refreshed, a week on Tuesday, she adds.

I thank her an for the first time I realise the enormity of the plague that I am about ter inflict on her an her kid.

She hands me a holiday form an sez, —Would you like a Jelly Baby?

—No wine gums? I ask.

—No, sez Bella.

So I decline an head back ter Smithy.

Bella offerin me a Jelly Baby shows me one thing: the casino's coinin it. Ternights takins could be a quarter of a mill plus. I walk past the Punta-Banco table. The Chinese are goin wild. That an Marjong are the big games for the Chinese. Punta-Banco is a card game. Yer gamble on the nearest ter nine an yer can bet on yerself or on the dealer. The noise they make an the excitement they generate can only be matched by one other occasion an that's Jamaican old timers playin dominoes.

It's one of them nights where time goes out the winda an yer don't have a chance ter sign up new members. Later, it quietens down a little an Smithy takes her mag out an starts readin about the lives of Stars. Every now an then she throws me a fact about Kylie Minogue or whoever. Then she's on ter the problem page. —Hey! she sez, —listen to this. She reads out a letter ter me. The gist of it is some girl passes her practical drivin test by allowing her examiner to shag her on the back seat.

I'm fallin about, laffin. —Smithy, I sez, —that test is not beyond you. I have a cunnin plan.

—Fuck off, she sez. —Should she?

—Wot? I sez.

—Tell her boyfriend about her and the examiner?

—Of course, I sez, —after all she was only doin it for him, wasn't she?

We're shaken out of our reverie by the sudden appearance of Bella.

—And how many new members have you two signed up tonight? she demands.

I open the signin in book. —Four, I sez.

—Four? she repeats.

—Four, I assure her.

—There have been seventy guests in today, she sez, —and all you have signed up is four new members?

Then she looks at the book an notices that it's Colin on the day shift that's signed the four up.

—For goodness sake, get your fingers out, she sez, in a not so nasty tone.

Yer gotta watch Bella cos she can be tricky. One time she comes out smilin an sez ter me an Smithy, —Keeping awake are we, team? Ever vigilant? Nothing getting past?

—No, sez Smithy.

—The Invisible Man on whizz couldn't get past us, I sez.

—Oh really? sez Bella, —well explain to me why there are right now two Asians on Blackjack who aren't on the computer. Sort it out.

Meric walks down the stairs an tries ter walk straight in. I collar him. It's an old routine, Meric's bin on the town an despite wot he likes everyone ter believe, he aint copped again. He's one of them sorta lads that wouldn't have women fallin at his feet if he carried around a bucket of oil. All he really wants is for me ter ring him a taxi while he sits on the couch in Reception chattin up Smithy.

—You a member? I ask Meric, already knowin the answer.

—Yeah, he replies.

—Name please? I ask.

—Where you bin all your life if yer don't know my name? he sez, an Smithy laughs.

—I'll leave this one to you to handle, sez Bella, an fucks off.

—Look Meric, I sez, —this is just a night out for you, but it's a career for me. Do yer wanna become a member or wot?

—Naw just a taxi, he sez.

96

Smithy rings The Voice (we call the City Cars girl The Voice cos we aint never seen her).

—One for the Global, she sez.

It's a good earner, taxis. For every taxi we order we get twenty pence off City Cars. Pennies yer might say, but it amounts ter two or three quid a night. An people like Meric always bung us a quid for helpin em.

As Smithy's on the phone, Geena walks out. Geena's a part time whore an full-time nice person. She gives me a ticket an I go get her coat, an expensive one as always. Wot did Smithy say about Geena? 'Aldi cans in a Sainsbury's carrier bag'. True, but I like her.

I give her the coat. She puts a five pound chip in the tip tray.

—Cheers Geena, I sez, —see yer soon.

An I'm back listenin ter Meric try an impress Smithy.

—Yer know wot they call me in Gorton? Meric asks.

—Meric? laughs Smithy.

—King Nailer, he replies.

—Oh a joiner, she sez.

An Meric croons:

'If I were a Carpenter
 an you were a Lady
 I'd nail yer ter the bed.'

He reminds me of Strange Steve. I think of Maurice the winda cleana an the sock an I wanna be sick. I head for the toilets, barely holdin it down. I get in an three of the Village people are in there adjustin their dress. I dive right into a cubicle an bend over pukin. The boys are in uproar.

—Ooh, manners, sez one.

Another sez, —Talk about lookin a gift horse in the

mouth.

—Give him a big tip, sez a voice I recognise.

There's nothin like a group of gay men talkin about gang bangin yer ter bring yer back to yer senses. I rise, wipin sick an snot from me face. I look in the mirra. *How the fuck did I get so old?* I remember the winda cleana, not Maurice, some other mouthy fucker, knockin at the door. So I go an answer it an he sez, —Is yer daughter in?

Me daughters five at the time. So I sez, —she's in bed, mate. Can I help?

—I've come for the winda cleanin money, he sez.

An it dawns on me, he thinks Debbie the wife is me daughter, an it tickles me.

So I walk in laffin. She's sat on the couch. I sez, — hey, the winda cleanas at the door an guess wot? He thinks yer me daughter.

A look crosses her face. An that's when the eleven year difference started ter matter. The clock of our relationship was on tick down from that point onwards.

Matt, the voice that I recognised, passes me a tissue an sez, —You're cryin, Dunc.

I look in the mirra an tears are crawlin down me face as slow as buses down Oldham street durin rush hour.

—Cheers Matt, I sez.

The first sign of a nervous breakdown is other people noticin that you are cryin before you do.

I get back ter me post an Meric has thankfully taxied inter the night. I look at me watch. Half an hour ter go. I've bin gone forty minutes.

—Soz Smithy, I sez, breakin inter the vernacular of youth.

But she's a mile away wid her head stuck in a magazine.

Next thing I know it's last spin an chuckin out time. We open the double doors, place the tip tray in the middle of the counter, an wait for the hordes.

I look over ter the Cash Desk. There's a line of winners, but not enough ter bother the casino profit. Julie the bargirl leaves.

—Goldstein dropped fifteen grand on AR2, she sez.

I know this is all on camera so I feign disinterest.

The punters are pourin out, mainly Chinese. They all want their coats first.

—ME, ME, ME, ME, ME! everyone's screamin.

An,

—TAXI, TAXI, TAXI, TAXI!

It finally subsides an I lock the door.

Smithy sorts Reception out while I check an lock the toilets an do the fire check. I rip me dicky-bow off an bung it in me jacket pocket. I sign the fire book an Bella sez,

—Good shift, ter me, meanin I didn't let no fucker in who shouldn't be in an I didn't keep out no fucker they wanted in. Accordin ter the Gamin Act we're not allowed ter let in any one that's drunk. But I'd be sacked if I ever turned away a big punter no matter how pissed he was. Me an Harvey in our time have carried em off roulette tables not knowin where they are or wot they've lost.

I walk ter the far end of the casino an check the bin shed. Empty. I take the opportunity an ring Karen an Steve. He picks it up after about half a ring.

—'We sang shang-a-lang an ran wid the gang', he sings.

—It's on. Get ter Chadderton now, I whisper, an hang up.

I start ter walk down the casino an me mobile starts vibratin. I whip inter the toilets

—Yeah? I sez.

—Wot number does she live at again? sez Steve.

—Fourteen, I sez, —the end one.

—Righty-whitey, he sez an hangs up.

I get back ter Reception an on the top of the counter are four cans.

—Wot's that? I sez.

—Casino did well, sez Smithy, —two Stones for you and two Carling for me.

—Stone for bones an Carlin for darlin, I sez, laffin.

Just as I fuckin said, they make a quarter of a mill, an we get two fuckin cans.

Smithy's emptied the tip jar an is countin it.

We have a ritual wid tips, we always leave two quid in the bowl an transfer the extra into a jar under the counter. That way it looks ter the punters like we're havin a bad night, an we get the sympathy vote.

—Guess how much? she sez.

—About forty each, I sez.

—Forty-eight thirty, she sez, —not bad.

—Cheers Smithy, I sez, takin me share.

—Press Club or Mamma's Kitchen? she sez.

—Can't, I sez, —got the day shift tomorra.

—Doesn't usually stop you, she sez.

An I tell her about me enforced holiday, in muted tones cos we're still on camera.

All the croupiers (apart from the poor fuckers kept back ter do the count) an the kitchen staff start ter congregate in Reception, waitin for Bella ter come an unlock the door. About fifteen minutes later, she arrives an waddles upstairs ter let us out.

Those that are headin for the Press head for the Press. The rest of us wait for our taxis or drive home. Smithy heads for the Press Club on foot wid about seven others.

I get the first taxi. It's Bing.

—Blackley or Monsall? he sez.

—Blackley Hills, I sez, an we amble off into a drizzly black Manchester mornin.

We're listenin ter Louisiana Cajun music.

—Yer know wot I've always wanted ter do, me ambition like? I sez.

—Pray tell, he sez.

—Go ice skatin in Central Park, I sez.

—Well do it then, he sez.

I settle back inter me seat, thinkin, real philosopher is Bing.

I get dropped off outside me flat. I go in, roll a weed an lie on the couch wid me weed an drink. Well kid, I think ter meself, it's happenin as we speak. Nothin I can do but sit back an wait. Gonna be a long night. Then I remember me mam's sleepers. I get em out of me jeans pocket. I sit down on the couch, pour a Stella, an throw back the tablets. Fuck knows what's in em.

I wake up about ten in the mornin all twisted on the couch. I get up an me neck is killin me. I'm back in at twelve thirty, enough time ter shower, shave an shit.

The rule now is no contact. I've already took the precaution of gettin rid of me mobile, so if Strange an Crazy ring I aint attainable. It's funny but I don't feel no nerves. *Whatever happens, happens.* I get some beans on toast down me an at eleven-forty, me normal time, I jump the 149 inter town. I like the 149 cos it goes through the Cheetham of me youth, an it takes its time. I get on an it's hammered. I pay me fare an I sit down next ter some girl who's tryin ter stop her baby cryin. I look out the winda an lose meself in thought. The bus stops outside St Alban's Church. There's one of them religious quotes on a placard outside:

'The Lord giveth and the Lord taketh away.'

Yeah, too true from where I'm standin, I think.

I've lost me kids, me house an me wife.

I look beyond the message ter where all the gravestones used ter be. They modernised it a few year back, laid the gravestones flat as pavin stones an cut down the trees. We all used ter play hide-an-seek in there as kids. Me, Macca, Rigga, Sellotape, Rafferty, Linda Carthy an poor little Sheila Grimes. An a think of this day when we was playin hide an seek. I wanted the toilet bad, so I went back for a piss an I noticed poor little Sheila couldn't find no place ter hide, so I pointed to this old dumped fridge, told her ter get in, an she did. I shut the fridge door an went off fer me piss. Anyways, someone said, 'let's go on Barney's Tip skimming cans instead!' an the game of hide-an-seek was forgot about. We went an we were gone for an hour then we all went home for tea. About half an hour later there was a knock on our door. It was Mrs Grimes lookin for little Sheila. I said, 'I don't know an that', an she returned ter searchin for the missin kid. Soon it was desperate, all the men out of all the prefabs out lookin. Then I remembered the fridge thing, but by now I was too scared ter tell anyone, I could get in trouble.

The police were called out an a young copper said, 'don't worry', to Mr Grimes, 'We'll find the little girl'. He was true to his word. Twenty minutes later he opened up the fridge door an found Sheila, as blue as his uniform. He carried the barely breathin body back through the prefabs, like a rag doll. Sheila's dad Tommy came runnin. He took his daughter from the policeman, wailin as he went. I couldn't describe the noise that that man made that day. She recovered fine but all me life I've bin haunted wid guilt. Many's the night I see her little blue face an rag body.

The bus turns onto Cheetham Hill road. I'm ten minutes away from work an here I am day dreamin about ghosts from the past. It's a sign an I decide I've got ter have a quick one in the Monkey.

So I'm stood at the bar in the Monkey. An who do I spot in the other room? Strange Steve an Bella. *Wot the fuck are they doin in there?* They're meant ter be outside the Global in nine minutes. I duck out, unnoticed, an head for work. Me hands are shakin like a dryin out alky. Second and third ghosts I seen in ten minutes. Me mind's turniped. I get ter the casino doors an Dave off the cash desk, an Kerry the Valet, are already there.

—No sign of Bodicea? I enquire.

—No reported broomstick landings, Kerry sez.

I lean against the wall. Me knees are jelly. I don't know whether I'm gonna faint or ejaculate.

—Still pissed, Drunk? asks Dave.

—Yeah, I sez.

A couple a Croups arrive an it's time Bella was here.

—Alright for her, int it? sez a Croup.

An tales of Bella's tyranny are unfurled.

I decide ter defend her, more for show than anythin.

—She's bin all right wid me, I sez.

—Yeah? sez the Croup.

An I know from his tone he knows somethin I don't so I raise an eyebrow.

—Look, Drunk, when you go on holiday next week they've got a man learning your job. And if he's any use they're going to use you solely part-time. An if you don't like it, you're out. Grow up, she's a bitch, he sez.

I'm fuckin gutted. Okay I'm about ter rob the fuckers, but wot the fuck happened ter loyalty?

As I'm thinkin this, Bella an Steve walk round the corner. He's got his best suit on an looks cool. Bella looks like she's bin ravaged by orang-utans.

—Who the fuck's that she's with? asks Dave.

—Looks like that Palmer fella from the Gaming Board, Kerry sez.

An this is music ter me ears. As far as I'm concerned he's Gamin Board, an them fuckers can inspect yer boxers for skids if they want, so whatever Steve sez goes.

We all say muted 'hellos' ter Bella, an Bella passes me the keys ter open up. Her hand's dead cold. She digs the key inter the flesh of the palm of me hand. I fumble it, it drops, an I pick it up. Then I open up the double doors an dash down ter turn the Reception alarm off.

1-9-7-6-3, I bang in. The beepin stops.

The staff troop downstairs, wid all the enthusiasm of Christians at the Gladiators away fixture. It's 12.40pm. The casino opens 2pm. Forty minutes before 2pm, the timer on the safe will allow Bella ter key in the combination. Bella an Steve stay at the top of the stairs as I instructed cos the camera don't reach up there.

—Duncan, she shouts down, —don't put the cameras on. They're being checked at two.

—Right, I shout up.

I immerse me head in the Reception diary as they walk by.

JIGGY-JIGGY

The Drunk rings Steve to say the job's on. Steve wakes up Karen. They dress, take a bag with Steve's Sunday clobber in it, jump in Karen's Punto and head for Bella's. They get halfway there and Steve yells, —AW FER FOOKS SAKE! And causes Karen to nearly run into the back of a dawdling taxi.

The taxi beeps.

—Fuck you an fuck yer Mother's lodger! Steve shouts after the fleeing taxi.

—Wot? Fuckin wot? says Karen.

—The gun, Babs, I left it in the parrot's cage!

They head back, get there, grab it from the cage, and finally get to Chadderton at about quarter past five. The key fits, and they're in. Steve goes through and notices the burglar alarm panel. He looks at it. And sees he's had a stroke of amazing good luck. It is not on. If the burglar alarm had sounded he'd of ran, he thinks.

They're stood in the hallway, giddy, and wondering what to do next. Then this dog walks out, tail wagging and barking:

—WOOOOOFFFFF.

Steve and Karen are charlied up.

—WOOOOOFFFFF. The Jack Russell announces its presence again.

Steve raises the gun and blasts it through the snout, putting a hole half the size of a wine cork right through its head an splattering the new telly behind in the process.

The sound from the gun is no louder than the banging down of a toilet seat. The dog's blood seeps onto the light blue carpet. Karen puts a cushion under its head, and the dog whimpers. Karen says, —Aah, probably remembered bein suckled by its mam.

And then it dies.

They cart the dog into a corner, and fling a quilt over it. Steve's singing,

—'Duvet know it's Christmas time at all?' as they cover it.

—What's that noise its makin? asks Steve, listening to this gurgling sound.

—Sounds like hot fat bein chucked down a toilet, says Karen. —Sorta 'Squibblediwish'.

Steve kicks it in the jaw to stop it.

—Now let's wait for the Bella the ball, says Steve.

They straighten up and wait.

The initial high of the break-in and shooting of the dog subsides. It's the early hours and every car passing is amplified.

—Wot if someone heard the shot? asks Kaz.

—Take a peek, says Steve, —see if yer can spot any lights on.

Karen does a bit of curtain twitching.

—Fuck all happenin, she reports.

Steve wanders over to the display cabinet. His hands are sweaty and itchy from the mechanic surgeon gloves he's wearing that have been supplied by Durie without Durie even knowing. —Gotta take these off, he says.

—Like fuck, says Karen, —no finga prints, remember.

—Fuck, says Steve, —all a wanna do is scratch me bollocks.

—Keep em on, commands Karen in a voice that Steve don't care for.

—'So macho', he sings. He picks up a pot elephant and looks underneath. —Wonder if these are worth owt?

—Who the fuck am I, David Dickinson?

Steve looks through all the documents behind the clock on the mantelpiece. He comes across a postcard and reads it intently.

—He he, he laffs, —got a boyfriend in Morocco.

—Let's have a look, says Karen, —proper Derdrie Rashid, aint she?

An they pore over some Moroccan lad's innermost feelings.

—Sez he's comin over at Crimbo, says Karen.

—Put him on the Crimbo card list, says Steve, slouching down on the couch. He digs in his pocket and pulls out his tin and starts rolling a weed on the bamboo coffee table.

—Keep yer eyes peeled Babs, he says to Karen.

—You done that weed yet? asks Karen.

—Wot's the hurry? asks Steve, —aint gonna go nowhere just yet.

Karen sits down in a chair near the double glazed window. —Wish the bitch would hurry up is all, she says. She checks her watch and then the clock. — Fuckin draggin like a night shift at Slaters Sausages.

Steve lights the weed and draws heavily on it. — Right, he says jumpin up an dimpin the newly lit weed on the head of a pot elephant, —we gotta keep alert. He moves up behind Karen on the chair, looks at his watch, then starts playing with Karen's tits.

—Stay alert, she says, and shrugs him off. She spots the joint and goes over and lights it. Steve follows behind and sits down next to her on the couch.

—For fuck's sake, keep still will yer, says Karen, — yer doin me head in.

Steve decides to pass the remaining time counting the pot elephants.

About thirty minutes later she arrives. She lets herself in, shouting, —Rusty baby, Mammy's home!

She hesitates and thinks something's wrong.

107

—Baybeeeeeeee, she shouts.

Steve's ready. From behind a curtain he grabs her. She screams.

Karen, who's got a Harlem Globetrotters balaclava on, tapes up Bella's mouth.

—Now be quiet an nobody gets hurt, says Steve.

Bella's whimpering.

—Apart from the dog, adds Karen.

They take her over to the quilt, slipping on blood and brains as they go.

Karen pulls back the quilt and says, —This is one we prepared before.

Bella wets an shits herself in fear. They sit her down on the couch. Karen notices a Renoir print over the telly.

—Hey! she says, —we used ter have one of them up in the home.

—'Baby it's cold outside', sings Steve.

Bella starts mumbling into packing case tape.

Steve walks over. He kneels before her. —You're a good lookin woman for your age, he says, —now listen, to me it don't matter, a pigeon's life, a dog's life or a human life. They're all about the same worth in my opinion. Now me, I'm the second biggest nutter in this room. Her in the Bala's twice as loopy as me. An if you don't do as you're told your kid goes under the quilt. An I'll plead not quilty in court.

Karen guffaws at this merry quip. —It's the best day out I've had for ages, she says.

—Now let me tell you, Steve continues, —I watched me mam die of cancer aged thirty-nine, so I don't mind if I get killed durin this. I mean it's gotta be better than goin down to four stone an screamin for mercy to a God who wears a Walkman. No, I get the casino money or you an your Bambino are gonna be jibbin the Pearly Gates come tonight.

It has the desired effect of inflicting fear an compliance into the mind of his hostage.

—You're not supposed to say nowt about us that's personal, like, calls Karen.

—Sorry, babs, says Steve. And then to Bella, —forget what I said about me mam.

—How much did you make tonight? asks Karen, removing the tape for a second.

—Who? says Bella.

—Don't fuck us about, says Steve, —the casino. How fuckin much?

—A hundred an ninety thousand pound, says Bella.

Steve and Karen dance about. They pop the tape back over Bella's mouth then do a fry up and get out the spirits.

—'We're in the money', sings Steve.

—Hey! Malt whisky, yells Kaz, —an American cream soda. Aint had that one before.

The party starts to swing.

—We should get a dog, Steve says, after a couple a malt de cremes.

—Aw can we, Babs? says a delighted Karen. She's sat cross legged on the floor at Bella's feet, trying to roll a weed on Bella's, Woman's Own. Steve joins her on the floor and he starts to strip her. She carries on rolling, unperturbed as he undoes her Ben Sherman and throws it over his shoulder. She's naked from the waist up, apart from a balaclava with Meadowlark's picture on it and a pair of finger hugging mechanic's gloves.

—Beltin these things, says Karen motioning to the gloves with her head, —yer can roll a weed widout getting any draw or tobacco up yer finga nails.

—You aint got no finga nails, says Steve, —yer bite the fuckin things off. Get wicklows if yer not careful.

Karen laughs and gives Steve a 'Fuck me daft' look.

Steve begins to massage her breasts.

Bella shuts her eyes.

—Watch if yer want, says Steve.

—Join in if yer want, says Karen.

And the next thing you know Karen is mastabating Steve. If Bella needed any more convincing that these two were the genuine article on the sociopathic lunatic front she was getting it now.

—It's funny wankin int it? says Steve, as Karen wanks him.

—Yeah, says Karen. —Why?

—Well everyone duzz it, he says, —yet nobody admits it. It needs somethin ter give it credibility. Like if they suddenly found out it was a cure for cancer everyone 'ud admit doin it an yer'd be able ter wank on buses. An if yer caught the eye of a girl sat opposite yer, yer could shout, 'Don't mind me love, I've got a growth.'

A panting Karen pulls Steve to her by the handiest appendage available.

—'Yer shake my balls an rattle my brain', croons Steve.

And they fuck on the carpet, in front of Bella.

After they finish, they sit down either side of her.

Karen lights the weed she rolled earlier and asks, —You got the Chaz?

—Gotta give this girl a bath first, says Steve, slapping the thigh of Bella next to him.

—We've gotta do wot? asks Karen.

—Not me, you Babs, Steve says, —she's gotta look respectable when we take her back.

Karen takes Bella upstairs to the bathroom.

—No screamin, says Karen as she takes hold of the tape across Bella's mouth.

Wuuuuuuuuuuuzzzzzz, the tape goes as Kaz gives it a strong tug.

Bella lets out a shriek.

—Better done in one go, says Karen.

Bella is stammering and stuttering:

—Buuuuuutttttttttttt.

—Sssshhhhushhh, says Karen in a caring voice.

Bella is sobbing.

—Listen, says Kaz, —all yer gotta do is wot yer told. If yer stay calm an do everythin we say, I promise no harm will come to you or yer kid. Understand?

Bella nods.

—Let me tell yer somethin, adds Karen, —I'm as frightened of him as you are.

Bella has a shower while Karen sits on the toilet smoking.

Bella dresses. Karen ties up her wrists and red-tapes her mouth.

—Soz about all this, says Kaz, —just doing wot I'm told.

They go downstairs.

—Right, says Steve to Bella, —yer've probably figured out by now that we're professionals. Do as yer told an you an your little girl dont get harmed. Cross us in any way an one or the other or both of you die. Understand?

—I've told her all that, says Kaz.

Bella's nodding her head like she's decided to follow their instructions to the letter.

—Do yer want a brew? asks Steve.

Bella shakes her head.

Steve pops Bella's mouth tape down.

—What time's the kid come home? Steve asks calmly.

Bella trembles. —Ten o'clock, she splutters, —don't hurt her please.

—Everybody does as they're told an nobody gets hurt.

They sit down and wait for Bella's daughter to come home.

—Quit a job as a security guard cos I hated waitin around doin fuck all, all night, says Steve after a while.

—Easy Babs, says Karen, —remember?

The Drunk's plan called for complete silence at all times possible. The only conversation with Bella and her daughter was to be on a 'need to say' basis. The Drunk had said that silence was more menacing than words.

Steve remembers and him and Karen enter into a menacing silence. Forty seconds later Steve says, —fuck me, girl, yer like yer pot elephants don't yer? I counted em, yer've got thirty-nine. That's more than Billy Smart's circus has got.

Bella's eyes are bulging. Tears of fear are forming in them like balloons.

—An wot's that cuckoo clock all about? adds Steve waving the gun about, —it don't fuckin cuckoo. Wouldn't want that cuckoo-in, mind, not wid my nerves, I'd end up shootin some fucker.

—Ssshhh, says Karen.

—Waa? Steve starts ter say.

Karen puts her finger to her lips and gives Steve a look.

Steve gets hold of her finger and gently bends it.

—Remember wot happened ter the last girl that shushed me? he says, smiling.

Tears stream down Bella's face.

At nine o'clock Steve an Karen start to tidy the house as best they can. They sit Bella on a chair facing away from the front door so if Bella's daughter looks through the window she'll see her mum in characteristic Norman Bates' Mother pose.

They've rearranged a chair to cover the dog's body from view and both take up position either side of the window.

Six minutes later and Steve asks, —What time she home?

—In fifty-four minutes, says Karen.

—Fuck this for a game a soldiers, says Steve, —I'm havin another drink. He wanders into the kitchen. — Only Pernod an Martini left, he shouts through.

—A bit a both, Babs, replies Karen.

Steve pours them one each.

They sit down either side of Bella, on two tables they've taken from a nest of tables. They're facing away from Bella and staring out the window, gazing intently for the snotter to come home. So intently that it catches them by surprise when Bella's daughter, Glenda walks in through the back way. She's confronted by the sight of her mother, mouth taped up, nodding wildly. Glenda looks at her mam and then at the strange people either side of her facing the other way and her foot hits something soggy. She looks down. The quilt has come adrift of the head of the dog.

—ARRRRRRRRGGHHHHH, screams Glenda.

Followed closely by Karen and Steve, with Bella nodding along.

Karen grabs Glenda, but she's a handful.

—Hold her legs, Karen shouts.

Steve makes a grab for her but gets kicked in the balls. They roll on the floor. Steve pins her to the carpet. Karen grabs the gun and puts it to Bella's head.

—Sit down kid or yer mother gets it, she says.

Glenda sits down. Steve ties her up.

—Listen kid, he says, —we aint gonna hurt yer. We're pro's.

—Dickhead, says a defiant Glenda.

Steve tapes her mouth up and flings her back down

on the couch.

—There, he says, holding his balls, —that was easy enough.

Karen moves Bella over next to her daughter.

Steve picks up a table leg that's come adrift during the rough an tumble. He walks over to the couch. Bella and Glenda look terrified.

Steve puts the leg in front of their frightened faces and says, —a bit a glue, that's all, an it'll be sorted.

Karen minds the girls, while Steve goes on a reccy. He comes back with a game of Scrabble. —Fancy a game? he says to Karen, —got time ter kill if nothin else.

And before long they're engrossed in a game of Scrabble, Karen keeping the score on a sheet of paper ripped out of the telephone book.

—Quid, says Karen, laying it on the table.

—That's slang that, not allowed, goes Steve.

—Well, what's that then?

—Yage? It's a drug that gives yer ESP, declares Steve, —the Amazonian Indians make soup out of it.

Steve and Karen continue their game of scrabble. Steve complains that he hasn't had enough E's and Karen says she that could do with an E now herself.

The game finally wraps up.

—Right, Daughter, me an yer mam are goin on a little journey. You stay put an yer mam don't get hurt. Understandingtons? Steve says to mum and daughter.

Glenda nods.

Steve stands Bella up, an takes the tape off her mouth.

He points at Glenda. —Her life. In your hands.

And he passes Karen the gun.

—If I don't hear from Babs regular, says Karen, —I blow her fuckin head off. Right?

—Yes, says Bella.

—Explain to yer kid then, says Steve.

—Glenda, says Bella, —do as they say. Everything will be alright, Mammy won't let them hurt you.

Leavin Karen to mind a tied up Glenda, Steve and Bella leave the house and head for Manchester City centre in Bella's car. Steve is still gloved up.

—Are yer gonna keep the gloves on at the casino? Bella asks.

—Why? says Steve.

—It won't look right, says Bella.

An you care? says Steve. —Listen bitch, don't try none of yer tricks, just shut it an drive.

Steve slings a tape on. It's Marc Bolan an T-Rex singing, *Ride a White Swan.*

The car pulls up at the back of the Conti as per the plan. Then Steve decides they've time for a drink. They go in the Monkey, and get a corner table where a vigilant man could observe all comers and all goers. Steve hasn't slept for three days and is running on cocaine fuelled adrenaline, so his level of vigilance is somewhat minimised.

Steve orders a pint of bitter for him and a fruit juice for Bella.

—You're drivin, he says.

Bella remains silent. She scans the pub for a friendly face. None forthcoming, she sits silently, as Steve pays for the beer.

—An yer own? he says.

The barmaid gives him his change.

Steve scans the handful of shrapnel she's just given to him.

—Fuck me love, he says, —what's yer own, a handbag an shoes?

He sits down. He couldn't have got himself more

noticed if he was in there wearing a pink suit trying to get himself an alibi.

Karen sees Steve and Bella drive off and rolls a weed. Glenda is sat on the couch, bound and gagged. Karen starts talking to her.

—We aint bad people yer know? We don't wanna hurt anyone.

Glenda nods.

—If I take the tape off yer mouth, yer won't scream will yer? says Karen.

Glenda shakes her head, and Karen delicately takes the parcel tape from Glenda's mouth.

Karen's got the gun down by the side of the Woman's Own she's rolling on. This rolling is a long drawn out process, cos crumblin weed with gloves on is a bit like eating a *Kit-Kat* wid the wrapper still on it, she thinks.

—Wot's yer name? says Karen.

—Glenda, says Glenda meekly.

—If you an yer mam behave yer selves yer both safe, says Karen, —we don't wanna hurt nobody.

A couple of minutes pass an Glenda says, —Please can you undo my wrists? I can't get any blood to my fingers.

And Karen, half stoned, undoes the rope and sits back, holding the gun.

—Now don't try nothin Glenda, says Karen, — remember yer mam.

Karen gives Glenda a five minute break while she finishes her weed.

Karen stands. —Right, she says, —time ter tie yer up an lock yer in that cupboard. Don't worry as soon as we're in the clear we'll let 'em know ter release yer.

Glenda stands up. Karen begins to speak. —Do yer

116

wanna go ter the....... she starts to say, when from nowhere the side of Glenda's hand knocks her backwards. She's blinded and goes hurtling into the display cabinet. Bella's pot elephants go everywhere. The gun is knocked out of her hand and lands by the body of the dead dog. Karen checks the kid. Instantly she works it out. The kid's script goes, 'Karate Kid Foils Armed Robbers'. But Karen has been an abused kid and a battered wife. Her face has acted as a release valve for men's violence for twenty years or more, and one thing it has taught her is how to take a punch. She's a kid again watching her dad drag her mam round by the hair, listening to *Dolly don't yer ever go away again*. She is up as Glenda picks up the gun. She delivers a boot to the fourteen year old's ribs and follows it up with a kick to the head. Glenda lies still.

Aw ter fuck an back, thinks Karen, *now I'm gonna have ter carry her inter that fuckin cubby hole.*

Steve and Bella arrive at the casino. Bella passes Drunk the key, which he immediately drops. There's muted laughter all round. Drunk bends down and picks it up from Bella's feet. After about four attempts he manages to get the doors open.

—Wouldn't let him be a water carrier in the Sahara dessert with them nerves, says a piss taking Croup.

Steve shoots him a look that says, *Under different circumstances you'd be sorry.* I mean where the fuck is the respect? Steve thinks. Cowardly cunts, feared stiff a this fuckin woman, callin her ter fuck, an then willin ter humiliate a mate ter please her. Steve looks at her but she is not responding, just staring into space and wheezing.

He gently holds her back, while everyone else, the Drunk included, walks down the stairs.

Steve and Bella wait for the motley crew to enter into the casino's inner door and move out of sight. Steve stares at the arse of a young worker as she shuffles past the Reception desk. —Nice arse, he says to Bella, complementing her on her choice of staff.

They can hear the Drunk go about his business downstairs, singing in the mirror and struggling with his dicky-bow. God, he sounds strung out, Steve thinks, better keep me peepers on him.

He turns to Bella. —You be cool, he says, —an every fooker's happy. You play the have-a-go hero an yer kid's dead. No snot off my conk, it's completely your call.

His little pep talk seems to have had the opposite effect. Her legs start wobbling.

He pats her bum.

—Now for action, he says, —tell the d-d-dickhead on Reception ter turn the cameras off.

An he's nearly fucking blown it. He nearly said, *tell the Drunk*, an he knew that bit was a fucking banana skin. Got ter keep me head straight, he says to himself, keep meself in charge.

—It won't look right, Bella tells him.

Steve gets well pissed off. —Neither will yer kid if yer don't do as I sez. He's getting a hard on with all this power play, —Tell him they're gettin repaired at two, he adds, through gritted teeth.

She hesitates.

—Fuckin do it, Steve says, —remember the dog. He blows in her ear.

It unnerves her and she shouts down:

—Duncan, turn off the cameras. Someone's coming to fix them at two o'clock.

—Right, shouts back a happy, helpful Drunk.

They slide down the stairs arm in arm. Steve lets go of her and winks as they pass the Drunk, who doesn't even look up. *Ever the consummate professional,* Steve thinks, sarcastically.

Steve hasn't ever been in a casino before and he's fascinated by all the lights, tables and machines. It looks fuckin mega, he's thinking, plenty of days to come in places like this for us, me an Karen can play every casino on the Med. It's a happy thought, and he smiles and nods as they pass some croupier setting up chips.

They pass the cash desk and walk into the office. Steve takes this big swivel chair and motions Bella to sit on this little stool thing on the other side of the safe. There's time to kill so he drums his fingers. He always does this when he's thinkin, he muses, an he don't know why. He watches her brushing down her uniform, and thinks, not a bad lookin girl for her age.

Then she gets all moody. —Why are you fuckin doin all this ter me? she asks.

—Doin wot? Steve says, wondering what happened to her posh voice.

—Putting Glenda an me through this?

—Fuckin money, he laughs, —wot you think for? Cos we don't like yer?

She's trembling.

—An wot assurity have I got? she mumbles.

Steve don't want any more discussion. Drunk said 'no talkin', so he's got to be brutal and shut her up.

—The only assurity in life is death, he says, —but what we got to gain by killin your sprog? Nowt in it for us. If we get away with the money, we're happy, but if we don't get the money, we got a lot to gain by killin you.

—An wot's that? she asks.

—Revenge, he says, drumming his fingers, —sweet revenge.

—But, she says.

He puts his finger to her lips an sezs, —I'm in

charge. Too many fucks spoil the brothel. He smiles wide at his own joke. —How long now till we can open the fuckin safe?

—'Bout twelve minutes, she says.

—Send for a vodka an tonic for me, says Steve.

—You'd draw attention to yerself, she says, — Gaming board can't drink on duty.

—'There you go baby', he sings in his best Buddy Holly falsetto, —'carin again.'

—I care shit bout you, she says through clenched teeth, —all I care about is me daughter. An if owt at all happens to Glenda I'll kill you. I don't care how I do it, but I'll get yer somehow.

And Steve sort of admires her, got guts this woman, he thinks, he'd take his hat off if he had one. But he hasn't, so he laughs in her face and says, —Mighty big talk for a one eyed fat man.

It's a line out of *True Grit*, but he sees it goes right over her head. People nowadays got no education, thinks Steve.

I'm behind the Reception counter. I've followed Bella's instruction not ter turn the cameras on. Carol the valet maid comes out.

—Wanna coffee? she asks.

—Yeah, I sez, —who's that wid Bella?

—Gamin board, sez Carol widout hesitation.

—I better keep busy, I sez, an begin to put the New Members inter alpha-numeral order. I'm thinkin, *We've done it. We've fuckin done it. The hard part is over. Everythin must be goin ter plan or the Police woulda bin here by now.*

The rest of the staff start to arrive. The doors are still locked to keep the punters out till two, so I'm up an down the stairs like a Stannah stair lift, lettin em in.

It's mostly croupiers, an them fuckers think they're a cut above, cos they can deal fuckin cards. International fuckin Snap dealers I call em.

I nod an let em in. I watch them traipse down the plush, hard wearin, Wilton carpet. Past the murals of great sportin heroes baskin in the glory of their greatest moments. Past the legally required *Gamblers Anonymous* sign wid the broken glass, where Solly Cohen ripped it off the wall, an hit himself wid it, after losin two grand at blackjack (A method that the GA should recommend cos he never came back).

I watch them turn by the cigarette machine (which only issues packets wid seventeen in an don't give change), an on past the oxblood leather settees to the security door.

I amble down, ignorin their grumblin, an open the security door an let them inter the casino itself. As usual, not a one sez thanks for me trouble, an I note that they're all bored shitless before they've even dealt a card or spun a wheel.

This buoys me sinkin stomach, because none of these fuckers would notice if a nine-foot bear came in tap dancin an blowin a bugle, unless of course he was a card counter.

I sit on the couch an await the next croupier ter 'bing-bong' his arrival. Me mind's all over the fuckin place. I mean wot has that daft bastard done? Are the kid an Bella safe? Is Karen okay? Are the police on ter us?

I want him ter give me a signal but I'm frightened stiff that some fucker'll notice if he tries to reply. I'm fiddlin in me pocket an twirlin me lucky chip, prayin that God sees my side of this, or is at least his usual indifferent self. I gotta find somethin ter occupy me mind before it blows. I twirl the chip some more. I

121

got it off me hero, George Best. He came in the casino once, an me heart nearly jumped out of me mouth. I'd seen this man make grown men gasp wid anticipation every time he received a football, an here he was before me. I wanted ter ask him a thousand things, but every man's entitled to his privacy, so I just said, —Go in please, Mr Best, an enjoy your evening.

Anyway about an hour later he comes out ter use the cigarette machine an he aint got no change, so he asks me do I have any, an I take five pound coins out of me tips.

An I go over to the machine an I get him seventeen Benson's, an he goes ter give me a tenner, an I sez, —No George, I owe you them.

An he smiles an goes back in the casino. Later, when he's goin, he comes over an puts a twenty-five quid chip in the tip tray an sez, —Thanks. He goes out an I find out from the croupiers that he'd got tattered like a King Edward's on the tables. I've kept the chip ever since as a lucky omen. An yer know wot I'd a said if a ever woulda bumped inter George again? I'd say, —George, yer a fuckin jinx.

It dies down a bit an I decide ter print a membership list off. We do this once a week for no apparent reason. It takes a couple a hours an no fucker ever reads it apart from me, Smithy an Colin, an we only read it ter see who can find the funniest name.

Steve's waitin, waitin, waitin. The magic twelve minutes elapse in a matter of seven hundred an twenty long seconds, and the safe is ready to be opened.

—10,9,8,7,6,5,4,3,2,1, says Steve —Houston we have lift-off. Open Sesame.

The door opens to Bella's fingers.

Steve whistles, opens his bag and says, —fill her up, pump attendant.

Bella begins loading the money into Steve's bag. A hundred and ninety four thousand, four hundred an seventy three quid. It's loaded in seconds.

Steve takes his mobile out just as the office door opens. His hand immediately leaps for his belt where the gun would be. But Karen's got it. He looks up.

It's only a maid.

She's got a tray in her hand.

—Two coffee's Bella, the maid says, and puts the coffees down on the desk. She doesn't bat an eyelid at the open bag of money lying next to em. She turns and leaves.

Steve's stunned for a moment, glad Karen had the gun because the maid would have been shot by now if he'd had it.

—Don't any fucker knock? says Steve, —fuckin bailiffs show more respect.

He rings Karen's mobile. Karen answers.

—Sweet as a nut, says Steve, —as cool as the drool on a hound dog's tool.

—Have yer got it? says Karen.

—Yep, says Steve.

—How much? asks Karen.

— A hundred an ninety four grand.

—Nice one, says Karen.

—How's the kid? asks Steve.

—Sorted, says Kaz, —not a peep. Went in the cubby hole like a little lamb.

—Let me speak ter Glenda, says Bella.

—Later, says Steve, —you'll see her soon. She's a little tied up at the moment.

He says goodbye ter Karen, and him and Bella prepare to leave.

I look up from the members list.

Steve an Bella are walkin through the casino, sayin nothin, an out the doors inter Reception.

—Duncan, Bella sez, passin me widout stoppin, — I'll be back in forty minutes. If anyone wants me, tell them to ring back.

—Rightio Boss, I sez.

It's all goin ter plan. We've jumped the last an we're trottin up the home straight.

Karen leaves Glenda and the leafy confines of Chadderton behind. She's soon sat in the bathroom of her maisonette nursing swollen eyes. She's got a piece of cold liver on them to take the bruising down, there being no steak available. She takes Steve's call telling her they got the money and her mood picks up. In fact, she's bouncing. Her and Steve have got nearly sixty-five thou each. Enough to go live in Benidorm and never worry about the Social or the police ever again. She goes to the window. She's a little bit paranoid. She realizes this because she remembers she's been treated at Park House for four years, ever since she thought people were following her home, and consequently stabbed the electric man with a carving knife. From her window she spots two blokes in an unmarked car. They're deep in deliberation. Karen watches them through the dirty nets of her kitchen window. She's certain they're pointing to her Punto. Time goes by and she considers her predicament. She has to go and meet Steve, and she can still see the two blokes, sat in a car, sharing a flask. They seem to be arguing. She gives up waiting for them to shift and walks out with her hood up and dark glasses on to cover up two black eyes. She gets in her Punto and drives off, heading towards Collyhurst Street, and noting in her mirrors that there are no followers. She goes up Rochdale Road onto Victoria Avenue East, drives past the Berkshire and parks up behind the Chain Bar Mill, opposite the Gardeners Arms.

At quarter ter two Sancho comes out to Reception. We open in fifteen minutes.

—Where's Queen Bee? he sez.

—Dunno, I sez, —she's bin behavin funny.

—How'd yer mean? he sez.

—Dunno, I sez, —told me ter tell yer she'd be back in forty.

—The office is locked, Sancho sez, —what are we going to do for the Cash Desk float?

—Dunno, I sez.

—What should we do? he sez.

—Dunno, I sez.

—Do you think perhaps we should ring someone? he sez.

—Dunno, I sez. Sancho fucks off inside widout thankin me for me help.

He's gone till it gets ter five ter two an then he's back an panicking.

—Drunk, get me the MD on the phone, he sez.

—Is that wise? I sez.

—Just do it, he sez.

I ring Global headquarters, which are situated in Salford. I get the MD's secretary on the phone an I put her through ter Sancho.

Two minutes later Sancho's out.

—Look, he sez, —we open as normal. The boss at the Comet is sending five grand in notes and change round. And they've sent for a locksmith. Help me here, Drunk.

An I like Sancho, so I do.

—Shall I turn the cameras on? I ask.

—What are they doing off? he sez.

—Bella said, I sez.

—Yeah, he sez, —sling them on.

An we open dead on two an the usual crew saunter in, jabberin an yellin. An I get on wid me job.

Mai Lei comes down the stairs wearin a skirt that's smaller than a midget's foreskin. Mai's a Philipino, about forty, an always pissed.

—Drunnnnk, she slurs, —Jiggy-jiggy?

It's an old pantomime we play out.

—No Mai, I sez, —old time dancin St Clare's Tuesday. You jig there.

—Nooooo, she sez, —Mai an you jiggy-jiggy. Make much laugh an babies.

—No jiggy-jiggy, I sez, —bad back. Doctor say no jiggy-jiggy till it's better.

—When better we jiggy-jiggy? she asks.

—Jiggy-jiggy all night long, I sez.

Mai goes laffin inter the casino.

Shortly afterwards casino security arrive. An shortly after that the police arrive.

Steve and Bella drive through Manchester City centre, turn up Oldham Road, and are headed for New Moston. They get stuck at the lights at Thorpe Road. When the lights finally change they head up Thorpe Road, onto Lightbowne Road then up past Moston Cemetery. Steve tries a joke to lighten the atmosphere.

—Guess who's the most famous person buried in there? he says.

—Allen, Larkin an O'Brien, says Bella, remembering her Irish upbringing.

—Who? says Steve.

—The Manchester Martyrs, she says.

—No, he says, all needly, —someone more famous than them.

—I don't know, says Bella, as they pull up next to Broadhurst playin fields.

—The man who invented the crossword puzzle, says Steve.

—Wot about him? says Bella, irritated.

—He's buried in there, says Steve, —yer know where the main gate is?

—Yes, says Bella wondering if this is part of the joke or part of the robbery.

—Well he's fourteen down an seven across from there, Steve says, laughing.

Bella stands staring.   —Can I get me bag out of the boot please? she says.

—Wot for? says Steve.

—A packet a tissues, says Bella.

—Yeah, no problemo, says Steve, —I've slung yer mobile by the way.

Bella's face drops.

Steve marches her across the sodden grass and around the muddy pitches. There's one or two games going on, on the far side.

This'll do, says Steve, stopping at a bench. He motions Bella to sit down.

—Cig? he asks, sittin next to her.

Bella takes one.

—Right, says Steve, —see that tower block over there?

—Yeah, says Bella.

—Well on the seventh floor there, he says, —is someone watchin us. An if you move from this spot before five o'clock he rings me or the Harlem Globetrotter an your little snotter gets offed. Understand?

—No, says a panicing Bella.

—You've gotta stay sat there for three hours, says

Steve, pointing to a vandalised bench, —if yer do your kid is safe. If yer wait till I drive off an start screamin for help, a man in that block rings your house an I aint responsible for the next bounce a the ball. Remember yer dog. This will be all over by half five, an yer'll be on *News at Ten*. Don't turn us inter child killers. Just sit an stay, an at half five scream yer fuckin head off.

Steve finishes his cig and shakes Bella's hand.

—Soz about the dog, he says.

Bella looks at her watch.

—Two twenty-five, Steve tells her, and he walks off.

Steve drives the three quarters of a mile from Broadhurst playing fields. He parks up the car as per plan on a little drive off Moston Lane East, called Lamburn. He's also been helpful enough to leave the door open and the keys on the seat. On display on the back seat, for whoever wins *fastest finger first,* is Bella's leather coat. He knows the car is not going to last more than five minutes before some fucker banjos it and its next appearance is burnt out in Bogart Hole Clough.

Time now ter ease up, he thinks. It's a ten minute walk from where he is to Chain Bar Mill, so he sets off, whistling. He's just turned onto Hollinwood Avenue, and about to pass the fish shop, when the roof falls in. *Where the fuck is the money?*

—AAAAAAAAA ARRRRGHHHHHH.

He realises he's left a hundred and ninety four grand on open display in Moston.

He's frantic, cursing himself, and he takes it on his toes, back to the car, huffing and wheezing. Twenty years of smoking's knackered him. His guts are churning, his throat's burning like he's a fire eater gone wrong. He bumps into this fat bastard walking a dog. He can't stop, he's gotta keep goin, he's prayin like fuck ter God.

—Watch it, dickhead! Fatty shouts after him.

Steve keeps running, but makes a mental note that if the coin aint there then Fatty gets the blame, and he kicks him ter death, and if he knew his plan, Fatty'd be fuckin prayin too, Steve thinks.

He gets back to Warbeck. He sees a kid maybe fifteen in a doorway. He spins him round.

—FUCKIN MONEY, he yells.

The kid shits it and starts fiddling in his own pockets. He thinks he's being mugged.

Steve throws him back in the doorway, and tear-arses off.

—Bastard, the kid shouts.

Oh they're queuin up, Steve thinks, runnin on at the pace a man carrying a bag of spuds could match.

He finally turns onto Lamburn. He's a physical mess, the blood pumping round his body forty to the dozen. He looks at the car. Still there. He slowly walks down to it. Attempting to get his breath, he blows a snotter out of each nostril to give his lungs a chance.

The car appears the same. He's just praying it is. He opens the door. And there is a God. It's exactly as he left it.

Kids terday no get up an go, Steve thinks ter himself.

He sits down in the driver's seat and takes five minutes and a touch of the powder.

He's shattered. He lets out a low wheeze.

—'Nobody told me there'd be days like these', he sings.

He picks up the money bag and heads back on up the Avenue at a crawl.

At the casino, the phone lines are burnin an I watch all sorts of bigwigs from Central office arrive. The first port a call for the police is Bella's. As it's all happenin, Khalid walks in, late as usual.

—What's up, man? he asks.

—Dunno, I sez, —Bella came in an fucked off. Police an every fucker's here.

—Cool, he says, —no fucker knows I'm late then.

He strolls in as if he's not a care in the world.

And in truth he don't. Not until twenty minutes later when he gets busted for possession of cocaine.

Steve an Karen are united outside Chain Bar Mill. They jump in Karen's car.

—Love you Babs, says Kaz.

—Wot the fuck happened ter yer face? says Steve.

—Kid got clever, says Kaz, —so I slapped her daft.

—No respect, says Steve.

—Worse news is I think the Police are stakin your house out, says Kaz, overtaking a bike and shoutin —WAAAANNNNNNNNKEEEEEER!

—'Oh the Israelites', sings Steve in a trembly voice.

—Two of em in an unmarked car, Kaz says, —it's got DJB as the first three on the plate so it's Collyhurst based.

—Yeah it's an unmarked car all right. But yer could be just imaginin they were watchin me flat, like when yer thought that fella was followin yer, an he wasn't, an yer attacked him in the lift, says Steve.

—Even if he wasn't followin me he was starin at me tits, says Karen defensively.

—He nearly lost a fuckin eye for the privilege, says Steve.

Steve puts the radio on. It's the Beatles.

—Wankers, he says. He changes the channel to the news.

It isn't pleasant news:

Police today announced the name of the man they'd like to interview in relation to the death of Maurice Fallon, 36, window-cleaner and father of four. He is Steven Tucker, 34, of Monsall Manchester.

—Fuckin lies, says Steve, —I'm thirty fuckin one.

—Wot do we do? asks Karen.

—If in doubt only one place ter head, Steve says, —the Drunk's flat.

—But he said no contact.

—Fuck wot the Drunk sez, says Steve. An he's thinkin, bad enough that fuckin Bella givin me orders, now it's spreadin. One or two people round here better buck up on the respect front, or I aint gonna be responsible.

He look across at Karen an sezs, —Drunk's.

She gets the gist.

They get to Drunk's flat. It's on the ground floor, somewhere down near Blackley Cemetery. Trust that morbid little bastard ter live near there, Steve thinks, I bet he's a season ticket holder at the crem.

Steve sets about practicing the noble art taught him in Borstal. He got six months to two years for burning down a nursery and he came out a fully trained burglar. You can't beat government sponsored education, he muses. He slips his gloves on and they nip round the back. He starts humming like the murderer does in *Texas Chainsaw Massacre*. Karen giggles.

—Only take a second now, Babs, Steve says, climbing onto the window ledge.

He decides to mickey the window light. It's piss

simple. He taps a screw through the wood, takes it out, inserts a wire and pushes it up. The window springs open. He slings the bag of money onto the Drunk's bed, laughing.

—Every dart a cuddly Teddy, he says, —you in first, Babs.

Karen hops onto the windowsill as Steve drops down, and he helps her through the window, slapping her arse and twanging her thong as she goes.

—You comin through? she asks.

—No fuckin chance, Steve says, —open the door an I'll see yer round the front.

He strolls round the front, carefully making sure he isn't observed. The Blackley Hills have eyes. Karen opens the door and he strolls in. They go in the Drunk's bedroom.

Steve picks the bag of money up. —Not made his bed, the scruffy fucker, Steve says, —yer can tell he's never done any time.

He throws Karen on the bed and goes to kiss her, his hands movin like a deaf and dumb speed reader's. She pulls away.

—Never mind that, she yells, —show us the money, Big Balls.

Steve decides it's time for a toast.

'Well a never felt more like swiggin the booze', Steve sings, —get us a drink, Babs, — we're gonna celebrate big style.

He watches her wiggle into the kitchen, and he strips bollock naked.

—CAN'T AMUMPLEFUMPH THE FINTH, shouts Karen.

—CAN'T HEAR YER, Steve shouts, slapping his knob to attention.

He's lying amid the money when she walks back in. Great minds think alike: she's naked too.

—Where's the drink? Steve asks.

—Aint none, she says, —just fuckin grapefruit juice an that.

—Only one thing ter do then, Steve says, smiling, and she jumps on him.

And they roll about and fuck amongst the money. All thought of what they're going to do next has gone out of the window in Steve's mind. For the next half an hour he does what he does best. He fucks Karen. Half an hour later, he springs up an shakes her.

—Tenko Kaz, he says, —we gotta get ter Billy's an get them passports. We gotta think bout getting to the Dam. Maybe we should leave the Drunk's share here.

Karen nips into the kitchen to get dressed. —CAN'T DEEFUMPH, she shouts through.

Steve's sure she's taking the piss.

He waits till she comes in dressed.

—What? he asks.

—Can't leave Drunk's share here.

—Why? Steve says.

—What if the Piggy-wiggies don't believe his story? she says, —they might search.

—Good point, Steve says. —We'll keep ter plan an give it Billy. But we better box clever.

Steve dresses in a hurry.

—Get me some bags, he says as he's dressing.

Karen nips in the kitchen and comes out with some Aldi bags. Steve starts to wonder how she knows where every fuckin thing is in the Drunk's flat. He makes a mental note to re-address the problem at a more convenient moment.

They divide the money carefully into four bags. Steve and Kaz have got a bag each with sixty four thousand, eight hundred an twenty four in it. The Drunk's bag has got sixty-two thousand four hundred and twenty four in it and Billy's got the bare two grand in his.

—What do we do now? Karen asks Steve.

—Get rid of the prints and that.

They begin to scour the room for fingerprints, starting with the bedroom and working methodically round. As Karen gets to work, Steve's thinking, in all the time I've known this girl this is the first time I've seen her with a Hoover in her hands.

Then they sit back on the bed, sweating, and proud of the job they've done. The place is spotless.

—Could start our own cleanin business abroad, Steve says, thinkin ahead.

—Fuck that, says Kaz pointing to the money, — that stuff means people clean for me.

They take a last line before leaving.

—Better leave a note, says Kaz.

—I'll write it, Steve says, an he takes the paper.

Steve's there a minute, pen in hand. He can't think what to write. It's the same with postcards, he reflects. —Here, you do it, he says to Karen, —but make it vague. No clues.

She ponders thirty seconds, then writes it.

—Read it back to me, Miss Reilly, Steve says in a posh voice.

She reads.

Drunk,
When you get this, ring us. You know the number.
We're off to see the Chinaman.

—Good work, Steve says.

They leave it unsigned.

Steve pinches the Drunk's Russian watch and his fake Helly Hansen coat and they head off for the Platting and Billy Kelly's flat in the sky.

The casino has bin emptied of punters by the police an meself. Not an easy task cos when a Chinese person's got a Marjong bone or a card in their hand then personal safety or the wishes of the police come a poor second.

As Mrs Li put it: 'Casino robbed? Hahaha, casino rob me every day.'

After twenty minutes of unrest we finally clear the foyer, losin a lot of our regulars ter Soames's round the corner. I wouldn't like ter be on their Reception terday.

Janette comes out to the Reception carryin a tray of cups. I think she's brought me a coffee till I notice the cups are empty.

—You're wanted in the office, sez Jay, —the police.

—Wot the fuck have I done? I sez.

—Interviewing everyone, she sez, —how'd you put your password into this thingy?

—I'll do it, I sez. I log her in an fuck off ter me Nemesis.

The Police have based emselves in the Marjong room. So I knock. A voice sez, —Enter.

In the room are two plainclothes police officers sat on two chairs on one side of the rounded table. — King Arthur late? I sez, tryin ter keep up a pretence of ease.

—Sit down, one of em sez.

I sit down. There's a deck of cards next ter me. I pick em up an start shufflin em, force a habit.

—I'm DS Waine, DS Waine sez, —an this is Detective Constable James.

I nod.

—What can you tell me about this mornin? sez James.

I shrug an sez, —Not a lot.

Waine sez, —Do yer always drink prior ter work?

—Wot? I sez.

—I was on Traffic for four years, sez Waine, —an you reek of drink ter me. I've heard every excuse in the book mate from 'There was sherry in the trifle' to 'I use gin flavoured toothpaste'. But no skin off my dick, son, it's your liver.

Fuck me, I'm thinkin, two sentences in from 'hello' an he's already nailin me to the cross.

—I, er, I'm goin through a divorce at the m-moment, I stammer.

Waine nods. He don't say nowt but I can see it in his eyes: he's got the beaten look that a divorced man never loses.

—Right, he sez, —you seen Mrs Chapman come inter work this mornin?

—Yeah, I sez, —she came from Portland Street wid some fella.

—Did you recognise the man she was with? he sez.

—No, I sez, —someone said he was from the Gamin Board. I didn't pay much attention.

As I'm speakin, I'm shufflin Kings. It's an old trick: place a King bottom of the deck, give the cards a good shuffle, then deal the King yer've placed at the bottom from the top. Waine's watchin.

—Would you recognise him again?

—Yeah, I sez helpfully, —in my job yer gotta remember faces an I can remember his.

Another twenty minutes of innocuous enough questions follow an then the door opens.

—Duke, someone sez ter DC Waine, —you'd better come and hear this.

An Waine an his mate fuck off out, leavin me sat there on me own.

I'm wonderin wot fuckin development has dragged

em away from our rivetin conversation an pray the money's safe.

I look over the desk an see me personnel file in front of Waine's vacated chair. I spin it round. I've just got time ter read Bella's assessment before Waine an friend return.

This is wot the women who I've just had kidnapped, an whose daughter I've had bound an gagged has said about me:

A likeable man going through personal problems at the moment. I have recommended that Duncan take a rest and think about his priorities.

An underneath it a sad face drawn.

It's sorta sweet, an I get a pang a guilt. I spin the file back round and pick the cards up again.

The pang has just about subsided when I get a bigger fuckin pang. Waine saunters back in an sez, — do you know Steven Tucker?

—No, I sez, an I drop the cards I'm shufflin.

—A might nervous aint we? he sez, as I pick the cards up. —A little less drink in the mornin's is wot's needed, an I ought ter know, he adds.

—Right that'll be all for now, sez James, —we might need you later and we might need you for I.D. For now WPC Doulton will take your statement, you'll find her in the Admin room.

I'm shunted out.

An I know it's on top. They're onter Steve, but that don't mean that they'll get me an Karen. We could head out ter Spain, look up her brother. We could even lie low, not see each other, the 'seen nothin, heard nothin, know nothin' approach. Set up tergether when the dust settles. Maybe buy a house near the seaside or somethin. Me minds runnin wild, an the alarm bells are ringin like there's a thousand tiny Quasimodo's havin a convention in me head. I wanna scream.

I go see WPC Doulton. She's in her early twenties, wid blonde hair an a strikin figure. She could be a kiss-a-gram apart from the lack of make-up. There must be thieves in Manchester who consider it a pleasure ter be arrested by this girl. I mean yer'd demand handcuffin. I sit across from her an give me statement. A bit a basic stuff about meself, how long I've worked at the casino, me movements on the day, an a description of the robber. I give as vague a description of Steve as I possibly can without usin the words 'don't know'.

That done wid, I return ter Reception. It's bein manned by Monique.

—Right Monny? I ask.

—Yeah, sortid an mint, kid, she answers, mockin me guttural Mancunian accent.

—Wot yer readin? I ask.

—*Wuthering Heights*, she sez in her normal Didsbury voice.

—Like it? I ask.

—You won't wind me up like you did with that Freud and Shakespeare nonsense, she sez.

—No, I sez, —I bin ter Howarth an that.

—Really?

—Wid the kids. Crossed the little bridge, seen the cottage an wondered round the village. Me an the kids even put a little poem in the visitors book.

—You didn't? she sez, an it could be me but I think I catch a look of admiration.

I snigger.

—Furck off, she sez.

I smile an think ter meself int it funny how people wid money can't swear proper?

Me shift comes ter an end widout much more ado. Rumour has run rife throughout the casino. I've heard everythin from 'Bella's done a runner with Palmer' ter 'It's a Tong financed robbery to get back at the casino, because late calls have been banned on the Roulette'.

Sancho comes out an asks how's things.

—Sorted, I sez.

He sez, —Thanks for today, Drunk, you were belting. Take off now if you want, and I'll see you after your holiday. And don't drink too much.

I'm gutted. I love this casino. An it's all ended cos of the want of a fuck, an a silly argument. Why didn't I just leave things as they were? Why didn't Karen keep her legs an mouth shut? Why did Bella make me apologise? It's bin the story of me life, never bin able ter take criticism.

I go inside ter the toilets. I stink a sweat an sick an snot an fear. I put me coat down over a chair an take me dicky-bow off. I look at me face in the mirror. An notice the Y shaped scar down me snotter. As I contemplate the ravages of age, DS Waine walks in. I start ter dry me hands.

—Where'd yer say yer lived? he sez whilst havin a lag.

—Blackley, I sez, whilst wringin me hands under the dryer.

—Blackley? he sez, like it don't sound right.

—Yeah, I confirm.

—Have yer ever lived in Monsall? he asks.

—Monsall? I repeat.

—Yeah, he sez.

—No, I sez, an start ter walk towards the door.

—Miles Plattin? he sez, an I stop in me stride.

—Yeah, I sez, —used ter live there.

—Thought so, he sez, —I recognised the accent.

He finishes pissin an don't wash his hands.

—An yer don't know Steven Tucker? he sez.

—I keep meself ter meself, I sez.

139

An it's gettin a bit like an episode of Columbo. The bastard's singled me out ter be mithered an any minute now he's gonna ask me wot make of slippers I wear.

—Ever bin arrested? he sez.

Me mind flicks back ter various incidents.

–Well, have yer ever bin arrested? he sez.

—Just for drink an that, I sez.

—Right, he sez, starin at me coat pocket.

—Wot's that? he sez, pointin ter me hip flask.

I show it him.

—Sort yerself out, he sez, —pop a fuckin balloon near you while you're carryin a tray a teas an we all get scalded.

An I smile. Cos I got his fuckin number. He's AA.

I turn an go back for me coat an things.

—See yer Monique, I sez.

—Look after yourself, Drunk, she sez, widout liftin her head from Kathy an Heathcliffe.

I walk up the stairs an out a that casino an I don't look back.

Steve and Karen head for Billy's flat, Steve's driving. Steve knows he's now a wanted man. He's a got a pair of dark glasses on and he's taken to talking out of the side of his mouth, as a bit of a joke to try to make Karen laugh. Karen seems a bit moody to Steve. He can't figure out what, but something's getting to her. He tries to cheer her up a bit. —Hey Babs, he says, — this is the most wanted I've ever felt.

It don't raise a smile, she just sort of raises an eye, and rests her knees on the dash board.

Steve knows something's wrong. And he thinks to himself, *if I'm bein pushed off any cliff, then she's handcuffed to me.* He needs to see the Drunk. He wants to know if there's any contingency plan.

—You okay? he asks.

—The time of the month comin up, she says, — sorry Babs.

And he thinks, I've gotta control this paranoia. Enough enemies out there widout turnin on me own.

—Where we parkin? says Steve.

—Do yer have ter ask me fuckin everythin? says Kaz, snappin.

—Easy Babs, says Steve.

—Behind Corpus Christie, she says, —an pull yer fuckin hood up. Half a Manchester's Police is lookin for yer.

They park up in a little cul-de-sac that's little used apart from by Council vehicles. It being Sunday, it's empty. They make their way to Billy's flat and do the prearranged buzz.

Buzz-buzz, buzz-buzz, buzz-buzz-buzz

It takes Billy time to answer. After a lot of deliberation he says, —who is it?

—Us, says Karen.

An maybe it's the seductive female voice, or maybe it's the bottle and a half of vodka that he's drunk, but he lets them in.

They don't risk the lift. They give it trainer up the stairs instead, stopping every other floor to comment on the varied atrocities visited upon the lungs by smoking. They finally get to Billy's door and he ushers them in.

—Gotta watch that nosy fucker opposite, he says.

They follow him into the living room, noticing the crucifix and Sacred Heart as they go.

—Nice place, says Karen, being girlie.

—Got any drink? says Steve.

At this point it's all very sociable in a Monsall kind of way.

Then Billy goes, —Stick yer money I don't want

141

none if it.

—Fuck Chinaman, says Steve, —what the f.....

But Billy interrupts him. —Me name aint fuckin Chinaman, he says, an they notice that he's pissed.

—Okay Billy just sit down, says Karen, —an tell us wot it's all about.

—I said no violence, says Billy.

—You seen the news? asks Karen.

—Wot's a fuckin dog? says Steve.

—Wot about the winda cleana? says Billy.

—Nowt ter fuckin do wid this, says Steve.

—I'm out, says Billy, —just take yer bag an go. I don't want nothin.

—Can't do that Billy boy, says Steve, —you're takin the money, full stop.

Billy jumps up and Steve pushes him down.

—Calm down, shouts Karen.

Billy grabs his heart.

—Urgh me art, me art, he goes.

—Yer fakin old bastard, yells Steve, and kicks Billy in the legs.

Karen goes over to Billy on the chair.

—Steve, she says, —pour three vodka an cokes an we'll talk about this sensibly.

—Billy be sensible, says Karen, —yer in it up ter yer neck whether yer take the fuckin money or not. Accessory before, after an fuckin durin, so take it an buy the budgie a new cage.

—Blood money, says Billy, —I don't want a penny.

They sit there staring at each other.

—What fuckin hope have yer of gettin away wid it? Billy says.

—We've got a plan, says Steve, —don't worry about us.

—Right, says Karen all business like, —where's our passports?

And Billy ambles off to get them.

Steve puts the two bags that are Billy's responsibility on the mantle piece, and finishes his drink.

Billy returns.

—Here, he says, —now fuck off. He throws the passports into Steve's chest and they fall on the floor.

—Pick em up, says Steve.

There's a look in Steve's eyes. Billy and Karen see it.

—Who the fuck do you think you are? says Steve, —I aint fuckin nothin.

Billy's quivering. All he's got to protect him is his God, and he knows sometimes when you pray God's not takin calls.

—Just go, says Billy.

—I aint goin anywhere till I get respect, says Steve, grabbing up his glass and filling it three quarters vodka and one quarter coke.

—Why'd yer kill the fuckin winda cleana? asks Billy indignantly.

—He missed the fuckin corners, says Steve, —what's it ter you, old man?

—He was a good kid, says Billy.

—He fucked Karen, says Steve, sneering into Billy's face.

—If that was the criteria for killin people, says the mad old bastard, —then half a Monsall, Plattin an Collyhurst ud be on conveyor belts at Charlie Stiles's.

Steve snaps, and back hands Billy. Billy's false teeth go flying across the floor. They land under an old fashioned display unit.

The Drunk Needs A Drink

I need a drink. I head for the Castle on Oldham Street, a nice quiet Robinson's pub where I can sit an analyse me position and maybe taxi it home after five or six pints. I'm on me second pint when I see a familiar an not unfriendly face.

—Buy us a pint, sez Rentadad.

—Alright, Renta, I nod ter the former Tommy Joyce now forever known as Rentadad. An I could of wept seein him at me shoulder cos it reminded me of more innocent times, when I hadn't graduated into the school of robbery an murder. Even his name, Rentadad was pure *Magic Roundabout* how it came about. An I'm in the mood to wallow in nostalgia so I recall the how of it. Tommy sees this advert in the 'In Touch' in the *Evenin News*:

> JOHN MOLLOY
> Anyone knowing the whereabouts
> of John 'Skip' Molloy.
> Born in Moston, last known address
> Halliwell lane, Cheetham Hill
> please ring.....blah...blah....blah

So Renta gives it a ring ter sell some phoney information or wotever. An he finds out it's Skip's long lost son tryin ter trace him. The kid's seventeen an he aint seen his old man since he was two.

Renta sez, —I've changed a bit. I wear glasses now.

—Yer always did, sez the kid.

They arrange a meet the followin Monday. At first it's all very tentative (I mean let's have it right, they've fuck all in common, have they?). Then twenty minutes later, Renta's mate, that low life, Rafferty walks in, an shouts over: —Skip, do you an yer mate want a drink?

An the kid is convinced.

Over the next eight month they take the little tyke for everythin he's got. His old girl's died an he's got no family left. Plus he's codded cos his mam's left him everythin. The only kith an kin remainin on the bargain shelf of his life are Skip an Uncle Raff. Sometimes life can be a real bastard.

Anyway all goes well for eighteen month. Skip won't talk about the past:

—Too painful an yer can't unbreak an Umpty-Dumpty.

Then one sunny day in Tenerife, Junior runs outta money. So they decide ter tell him El Truth.

—Listen kid, says Renta, —I'm a con man (givin his self a trade that not many have seen evidence of), I aint really yer dad.

An the kid only smiles an sez, —Yer me dad as far as I'm concerned.

An the daft thing is that they only take him inter their little gang an teach him all they know. So much so that six months later they give him six ton ter buy a van an he only fucks off wid that an Renta's live-in, Hillary.

—A chip off the old block, sez RentaDad, an moves Hilary's sister Gretal in.

Which I suppose yer could say was a fairytale endin in a Collyhurst kinda way.

I buy Renta a pint.

He's his usual gregarious self.

—Yer lookin mellow, he sez, —here you know a thing or two, Drunk, yer know like if yer have sex on a plane yer in the mile high club?

—Yeah? I sez.

—Well wot are yer in if yer have a gobble in a

Butlin's monorail?

—A class of yer fuckin own, I sez.

We have a couple, then he suggests a pub he knows near the Daily Express in Ancoats.

—Got strippers an novelty acts, he sez by way of recommendation.

I aint got nothin ter go home to apart from worry an misery, so I agree.

We get there an there's an advert in the winda advertisin tonight's act. *Anna Condor and her Condor Moments.* I can't help thinkin from her promotion picture that her moments have bin an gone. I pay a fiver each in. The place is fuckin heavin. Renta goes to the bar to get the beer in an I stand near the door listenin to all the shoutin. I'm standin alone an Rafferty spots me an strolls over.

—RIGHT DRUNK, he bawls down me ear even though there aint no need cos the music aint that loud.

I wince but he shouts,

—SHE'S SPITTIN PING PONG BALLS OUTTA HER TWAT. IT'S LIKE ANCOATS LADS' CLUB ON A BLIND NIGHT.

I laugh but not as much as he does.

Renta comes back wid me pint an Rafferty shuffles off.

—Wot did he want? sez Renta.

—Nothin, I sez, —you two fell out?

—The man's a cunt, sez Renta.

An he tells me the root of the antipathy.

I get another round in before the cabaret comes out for the second half an I find they've put a pound on the price of a pint ter cover the act. Still, I think, ping pong balls don't come cheap.

It turns inter one of them beltin nights. I stand on the back of a chair to get a better view of the second half. The audience love it, me I've seen three of me kids born, so wot a woman can or can't get up or down her tunnel of love is no mystery ter me. The novelty act finishes an me an Renta grab a table against the wall. Rafferty stays at the bar. Most of the crowd drift off.

—How'd you fancy bein married ter that Anna Condor? Renta asks.

Are we havin another here? I ask.

—Naw, sez Renta, —fancy Bookkeepers?

—Yeah, I sez, —a while since a bin there.

It's got a nickname 'Fuckseekers' on account of the general ambience of the place. We're just on our way out an Rafferty collars me.

—Quick word, Drunk, he sez.

—Wot? I sez.

—Seen yer today, he sez smilin.

—Well? I sez.

—In the Monkey, he sez, —yer bobbed in, seen Strange Steve an bobbed out. They want him for murder yer know?

—Look I gotta get goin, I sez, me nerves startin ter jangle.

—Lend us twenty quid? he sez.

An I'm too cabbaged to tell him ter fuck off.

—Cheers Drunk, he sez an turns.

I walk out an see Renta pissin against a Peugeot.

We get in Bookkeepers after givin the bouncer our assurances that we won't trouble his night. We walk past the cloakroom an head for the fairly crowded bar an order a bottle a piece. There's two spare bar stools, facin the entrance, so we avail ourselves of them. We sit watchin every pair of legs comin down them stairs. It's a must Bookkeepers is, for every divorced sod in Manchester. It's got one big dance floor downstairs that covers three rooms an there's a room at the bottom, wid booths in it, where yer can either grab a grannie or grab a burger or grab both. Then there's all these huge statues of different people, who I can't quite make out. One looks a bit like Elvis on a day when he hasn't had his medicine or maybe when he's had too much.

Yer don't get much trouble cos most of the clientele would rather have a bowl of pea soup than a fight. An even if yer don't cop, yer at least get ter think yer've got half a chance. In some ways it's strangely life affirmin, we're all relivin the school discos of our teenage years. The tune blarin out as we get served is, *Walking Back To Happiness* by little Helen Shapiro, an it's a particular favourite of Renta's. I look round at him an he's up on his stool, clickin his fingas above his head, singin an boppin along.

Plenty of life in the old warhorse yet I think, an sing along.

I look around the place. It's evens, men an women. We buy a bottle apiece an sit at the bar watchin. After twenty minutes two married women out for a bit of fun stroll in. They make their way ter the bar an we let em have our barstools. I get em a couple a lagers an a brandy an lemonade each. We start chattin. After half an hour, my one, a short, tubby girl wid tits, is tellin me, 'me husband only seems to want anal since he turned forty. He don't want it normal, an that aint normal.'

—Bet yer don't know which way ter turn? I sez. We giggle tergether, her head leanin inter mine. — Where's he now? I add, lookin round defensively.

—In Cardiff with the kids, she sez, wipin somethin off me bottom lip wid her little finger.

An she tells me her life story in thirty well-rehearsed seconds.

—Married in haste, repented at leisure. Babies at seventeen, nineteen, twenty an twenty four. First husband fucked off with the secretary of the local Rugby club. Now married ter a man who grows Christmas trees. —An you? she sez.

I give her the usual drivel.

I look round an Renta's dancin. His hands are everywhere. I notice his bird is a bit lackin on the tit front. Probably a sacrifice ter the God of kids. I nod at Renta an he winks back. We're in the home straight. I look mine in the eyes an muster up what dregs of sincerity a can find in the sewer of me heart.

—Janice, I sez.

—Janine, she corrects me.

—Janine, I sez, —do you fancy comin back ter Renta's? I'd like ter get to know you betta.

—As long as it's proper, I don't want no more of that arse business, she sez, an she lets out this whinin laff. I pull her to me, more ter shut her up than out a lust, an I put me hand under her top.

Renta an his girl, Samantha, are dancin ter, *Brown Eyed Girl*.

—Let me get Sammy, sez Janine.

I watch her walk away, her arse bulgin in white jeans that must a bin sprayed on. An who could blame her old man for parkin his bike between two such lovely bollards?

Renta returns, he's got a hand on each arse. I gotta watch the tricky fucker cos I can tell he's after Janine an I'm gonna be palmed off wid Sammy.

We finally arrive at Renta's flat at the back of the Admiral off Rodney Street. Renta goes for four glasses an a bottle a vodka.

To keep the girls entertained, I tell em I've met Oasis.

—What are they like? asks Sammy

—Shit, full of emself, Scouse tribute band, I sez.

—Yeah but are they hung like donkeys? asks Janine.

—I'll be your My Little Pony, I sez an join her on the couch.

Renta returns wid four vodka an ginger ales, two of em heavily laced. I take a gulp of mine, nearly burn me throat out, then I realise it's three of em heavily laced. I know his game. Janine is the best lookin girl either of us has copped for in a long time an he's after her.

I walk over to his tape deck. Fuck all worth listenin to. It's either the Eagles or the Sex Pistols. I sling the Eagles on. Renta meanwhile has rolled a spliff to ease the already comatose atmosphere.

I'm just gettin comfy strokin Janine's growths, savourin the warm taste of vodka an ginger an thinkin, wot the world needs now is love sweet love.

The Eagles are singin, *Desperado.*

Me mind starts ter wander ter where the Desperados are. I'm a cowardly bastard. I've stayed as far away as possible. I tell meself it's the plan, but it aint, it's cowardice.

I'm just about ter freewheel inter depression when Janine sez, —Shall we dance, Sammy?

Sammy sniggers an sez, —See what the boys say.

Janine, who by now has moved onter me lap, adjusts her arse on me dick an sez, —Do yer wanna see a lesbian dance?

—Wot, no Scrabble? sez Renta, laffin.

An the pair of em start. First Janine strips off Sammy's top ter reveal two undersized yet well formed little tennis balls wid studs through the nipples Then Sammy strips off Janine. I feel like Livingstone gazin on Victoria Falls for the first time. She's got the best pair of tits outside of Fantasy Island. Sammy pulls Janine's tight white jeans down to her ankles, an it's just a thong at twilight. They both get naked an simulate intercourse. Renta can handle no more. He strips off with all the speed of a man jumpin in a canal ter save a drownin kid, an jumps down between em.

The snidey fucker makes a play for Janine but I get in between him an Janine an bury me head in the mound of her tits, an I just hope that's an elbow I can feel stickin in me back.

In wot seems like an hour later but is probably about three an a half minutes, I'm ready to shoot. She's got her legs wrapped round me back an she's pullin fuck out of me hair. I look over at Renta an he's givin it Sammy from behind. I never realised before how well hung he is an I get a bit jealous of all the screamin he's makin her do.

—Nice to hear someone's enjoyin themselves, sez Janine gigglin, as I empty me sack inter a willin receptacle.

A look of disappointment crosses Janine's face. Like a woman at Bingo who bought the book after the jackpot winner bought hers. I lie there breathless. Renta pulls outta Sammy, pushes her on her back an plunders her mouth wid his weapon. She slurps an squeals.

—Swallow, he sez.

—One don't make a Summer, I call out, an go an get me an Janine another fire water.

As I return wid the drinks I see Renta slippin in beside Janine. He's unbelievable. He's hard again already. He turns Janine over. —This'll stop yer gettin homesick, he sez.

An he pushes in wid all the tenderness of a double glazin salesman. Sammy's lay there pantin. Oh well, I think, any marina in a drizzle.

I wake up wid a bouncin headache. I look at me watch. It's quarter past six in the mornin. I look over at Janine. She's naked apart from a coat pulled over her legs, an all yer can see is a mountain a fat. Her mascara's ran so she looks like a giant panda. I tip toe to the door. Renta lifts his head.

—Where yer off?

—Bottle a milk, I lie.

I get outside. It's rainin. I trot down Livesey Street an jump a 64 on Rochdale Road. I get off at the junction wid the Avenue an walk the quarter of a mile in the wind an rain.

Thank fuck I aint got work. I figure if it's all on top then the police'll be sat outside me flat waitin for me. An if the plan is still functionin there'll be a simple message on me answer phone sayin, —This is Billy. Fancy a drink? That means: 'I've got your share of the money and I've put it in my loft as instructed'.

I get to the flats an there's not a soul about. I put me key in the door an I go in apprehensively.

When I go out I always leave a matchstick propped against the top of the livin room door, then if it's on the floor when I get in, I know someone's opened that door.

The matchstick's on the floor. Shite. I know someone's bin in or still is in. Me first thought is the police.

I get a hammer out of the electric cupboard an open the livin room door slowly. Nobody about, so I go room ter room. I find a note from Steve an Karen on the bed.

An it aint bad news.

—YEEEEEEESSSSSSSS, I yell.

I'm made up. They've got the wedge an they've given it Bilbo, that'll do for me.

I sling the kettle an the toaster on, an go ter listen

ter me message machine.

Billy is on the chair looking at his teeth under the cabinet. —Pass us me teeth, he says to Karen.

—Yer what? says Karen.

—Shut the fuck up, gummy, says Steve, —I'm thinkin.

Steve's staring at the top of Billy's head. —Sufferin wid dandruff old man, he says.

—A might have dandruff, Billy replies defiantly, — but the sufferin's minimal.

Steve sits down on a chair opposite Billy. Karen leans against the wall.

—Ring Drunk, says Karen, —he'll know wot ter do.

—He won't be home for another half an hour, says Steve, —gag the old bastard an we'll wait.

Karen gags Billy. And pulls out a little packet of happiness from her pocket.

—Steve, she says, —Eskimo time. Gotta chill out, Babs.

They give it half an hour then leave a message on Drunk's answer phone. Steve has recovered his high and is gettin all chitty-chatty. Karen is chopping some more of the stuff that Billy thinks looks like icing sugar.

—What's the problem, Chinaman? Steve says to Billy.

But Billy can't answer because of the gag.

Karen takes it off his mouth.

—Quiet now, she says, —no more shit.

Billy sits there and listens to Steve's life story.

—I remember one day when I was a kid, begins Steve, —I'd absconded from Approved School with this kid from Salford, Charlie Marley he was called. We'd made off after lights out. No big deal, just out of a

153

winda an inter the real world. We got caught the next mornin in a field near Marple. When the police turned up they found us throwin apples at cows. I remember sayin ter Charlie 'Has yer mam got a black an white coat?' An he says 'No', an I sez, 'Oh it must be a cow in that field then'. He chased me inter the arms of a local Copper, who slapped us an took us back. That afternoon we were placed in a room, sat on two chairs, told not ter talk, an we watched the other juvenile delinquents play football in the yard. We couldn't move or look at each other, just watch. About an hour later the night screw, Jolly comes in, 'Face front', he screams. 'No little wanker fucks up MY night shift an gets away with it' He's pacin up an down behind us, then, Bang, a knuckle crashes down on the back of me head. 'In every gang there's a leader an YOU'RE IT, Tucker', he sez. I hear a sigh of relief escape Charlie's lips. Jolly makes me stand up, not by askin, but by pullin the roots of me hair. An he punches me between the shoulder blades. 'YOU can't beat authority,' he sez an punches me in the ear. I fall like a tree beneath an axe. He makes as if ter kick me but thinks better of it. I hear him laffin. 'Not so tough now are we?' he goes. His thinkin better ends. A steel capped shoe shakes me ribs. 'You'll learn Tucker,' he sez, 'you just can't beat authority.'

—My poor Baby, says an emotional Karen.

Billy says nothing, but his face is saying he's heard these sort of whining shites before, everybody's fault but their own.

—Give the Drunk another ring, says Steve.

Karen leaves a second message on Drunk's answer phone.

—He's still not there, she says.

Steve gets a hold of Billy's shirt, pulls him to him and slaps him. Blood trickles down Billy's face.

—Just take the Drunk's money an we go, says Steve.

Billy spits blood back at Steve.

—I aint gettin involved, says Billy, —I told Drunk 'no violence'.

—ARRRRGHHHH, wails Steve, and pulls the gun out of his waistband.

—NO, shouts Karen, —let's go. Fuck him. We'll keep the Drunk's money till we see him. Calm down, Babs.

Steve sits with his head in his hands. Calm is struggling to make it onto his agenda.

Billy weighs up the situation and takes a calculated risk.

—Listen, he says to Steve, —I've known you since you were a kid. An yer've always bin a bottleless bastard. If the Drunk wasn't bombed out on depression he wouldn't waste his time wid a loser like you. Now take yer money an yer woman an fuck off. Yer don't frighten me. An yer never will.

BANG, Steve blows a hole in Billy's thigh.

Billy's calculated risk has come unstuck.

—At the third stroke, says Steve, as Billy hits the floor, —you will be dead.

There's blood pumping from Billy's thigh, the bullet's hit an artery or something.

Karen rushes for a towel. There's a knock at the door. Steve bangs the telly on full blast. They wait a second. There's another knock.

—Answer it Kaz, Steve says.

Karen opens the door a little and it's the woman from across the hall.

—Is everything all right? she says, —I heard a noise.

—Just the telly, says Kaz.

—Is Billy in? says the nosy neighbour.

—Asleep luv, says Karen and shuts the door.

Things are bad with Billy, blood's pumping everywhere.

155

—Ring the Drunk, says Steve.

—Fuck the Drunk, says Billy, —ring a fuckin ambulance.

Steve motions to Karen and Karen rings the Drunk while Steve gags and binds Billy.

—It's his ansa again, says Karen.

They sit down in silence and Billy slips in and out of consciousness.

—Why? says Karen, —we coulda just kept the money.

—He wouldn't obey The Plan, says Steve, —an this can't work widout The Plan.

Sometime about three in the morning, Billy dies.

I sling the answer phone on. The voice sez:

—You have eight messages.

I sez a quick prayer an tap the play button.

—Message One

—Hi Ya Dad (an it's Shannon)......... Are yer there Dad?....... Dad are yer havin us this week? Let me know cos me mam sez yer can if yer want ....See ya.

(I delete it)

—Message Two

—Drunk, pick it up, it's me (Steve)......... I gotta talk ter yer....... It's important...... If yer there pick the fucker up.

(I delete it)

—Message Three

—Mike you there (it's me mam)? Your casino's bin robbed. Are you alright? Ring me an let me know.

—Message Four
—Right pal (it's Macca), just seein if yer goin for a pint termorra an that...... Let me know ......see yer.... bye.

—Message Five
—Drunk it's me, Karen..... Don't fuck about, if yer there pick the phone up ......We got problems...... Drunk.... Pick up the fuckin phone...... I can't control what's goin on much longer.... Pick the phone up.
(I delete it...... Me hearts in me mouth, it's like a play unfurlin in front of me).

—Message Six (Is an anti climax)
—Brrrrrrrrrrrrrrrrrrrrrrrrrrrrrrrrrrrrrrrrrrrrrrrrrrrrr (the phone sez..... so I delete it)

—Message Seven
—Steve's shot Billy (sez Karen an me stomach somersaults inter me chest) ....Don't panic it's not serious (How the fuck can shootin someone not be serious?) ....It's only in the leg ......He's bleedin a bit....... Might need a stitch or two.......... Drunk?... We need yer...... Get down here....... Whatever time yer get home ring our moby.................. Please....... Don't let me down...........

—Message Eight
—..........(Silence).......... Drunk, Billy's dead (It's Karen) ....He went about ten minutes ago ....(Silence)........ He bled ter death........... Nowt we could do........... Ring our mobile as soon as ....WHERE THE FUCK ARE YER? (Steve takes over) YER SHOULD BE HERE........ ...YOU FUCKIN WANKER..... IT'S US GOTTA DO THE DIRTY WORK............... .(Silence)................. What do yer

157

want us ter do wid your share?

I press the delete button an fall back inter me chair.
It's turnin inter a blood bath. Why the fuck did I go
on a bender wid Rentadad? If I'd a bin there a coulda
stopped it. I can't fuckin figure it. Billy's on our side.
All they had ter do was give him a bag a money an
get their passports. Fuckin Billy, I think, I bet he was
holdin out for more money. Wanted ten grand apiece
for their passports. Greedy fucker deserves it. He
should of known better than mess wid Steve. I look at
the clock an it's quarter past eight. Ter think this time
yesterday me only worry was me divorce.

I ring Karen's mobile usin a pay as you go mobile
I'd picked up specially. I'm beginnin ter think them
an God are takin the piss out of me. I get the answer
phone. I start ter leave me message an Steve picks it
up.

—'I'm all shook up huh huh', he sings.

For a moment I'm lost for words.

—Why? I finally say.

—What? he sez, laffin, an this I don't need.

—Right I need ter know everythin that's happened
to yer from gettin ter Bella's to pickin up this phone
call. Leave nothin out.

He tells me the comedy of errors that have befell
him an Karen. An somethin strikes me. If I'd a done
the casino wid any other fuckers than these then it
woulda worked. The plan held up, the hypothesises
was correct, it's just that the white mice have failed
the test. I'm workin wid inferior white mice.

I listen it through, then I sez, —The winda cleana
I don't understand, the fuckin dog I don't understand,
Billy Kelly I don't understand. Wot the fuck yer doin?

—Fuckin Karen, he sez, —what you doin?

—Steve, I plead, —why?

158

—It's just the way things went, he sez.

—Yer sick, I sez.

—I'm sick? he sez.

—What's yer game plan now? I ask.

—Hole up for a week or two, he sez, —let things die down an fuck off ter Spain.

—What do yer want me ter do? I ask, prayin he don't wanna meet me.

—Gotta meet yer, he sez, —give yer what yer've got comin an that.

—When? I ask.

—In a couple a days, he sez, —are they onter you yet?

An I don't like the use of the word 'yet' in that sentence.

—Dunno, I sez, —just keepin me head down. They're bound ter come round here.

—Right, he sez, —I'm throwin this moby. I got a new one, take this number down.

I take the number.

—Yer the only one that's got it, he sez, —so on Wednesday at four you ring us an we'll tell yer where ter meet.

—Right, I sez thinkin, *like fuck*.

—Oh, he sez, —sorted Durie out for yer.

—Aw for fuck's sake, I sez, —yer've not offed fuckin Jukebox as well.

He's laffin down the phone. Long blasts of belly laugh like a man who aint got a care in the world.

—No, he sez, —we've left Karen's car parked in his lock-up an give the police an anonymous tip-off. Changed the padlock, so it'll look like he's bein awkward when he don't open it. Left a pair of gloves we found in there in Billy Kelly's flat. That'll teach him fer openin his mouth about the Imaginary Loads. He had it comin.

159

An despite the circumstances an the fact that Billy's dead or maybe because of all that, I find meself laffin me balls off.

—Ring Wednesday, he sez.

—Will do, I sez.

An I think ter meself, I daren't not.

—See ya, he sez in a cheerful voice.

I hang up. I aint bin off the mobile twenty seconds when the land line rings. I don't pick it up cos if it's the police I need time ter study me next move.

'Hello we can't take your call at the moment   but if you'd like to leave your name,   telephone number and a short message   we'll get back to you as soon as possible.'

—Hello it's me Macca, the voice on the other end sez.

—Yeah, I sez, —sorry I was in the kitchen doin a.......

He interrupts.

—What's goin on?

—Marvin Gaye, I sez. Your turn: who sang, *Tears of a Clown*?

He's havin none of it.

—What the fuck's goin on? he repeats.

—What d'ya mean? I sez.

—What do I mean? he sez, —what the fuck's happenin?

An I realise it aint no use tryin ter fob him off.

—Macca yer don't wanna know, I sez.

—Fuck off, Drunk, he sez, —we grew up tergether.

An I honestly don't want ter drag him inter this sorry fuckin mess. I mean Macca's a big lad who can handle his self but this is uncontained an uncontrolled insanity.

—I swear yer don't wanna know, I sez.

—How soon before every fucker knows? he sez.

—What do yer mean? I sez for the umpteenth fuckin time.

—You aint gotta be a mathematician ter get four out of a couple a twos, he sez, —your the link ter all this.

—Leave it Macca, I sez.

—Leave it? he sez, —Chinaman's dead. Maurice Winda's is dead, your casino's bin banjoed. Strange an Crazy are doin a Bonny an Clyde all round Plattin an as far afield as Monsall. How soon before some fucker explains that you're the common denominator?

An I start ter think he's bin helpin his youngest wid his homework, cos all I'm hearin is maths analogies.

—It's nothin ter do wid me, I sez.

—WHAT? he shouts an it startles me.

—I dint get involved, I sez, an I hear him sigh.

An it's like I'm a kid again at confession. I just gotta get it off me chest.

—I just told Steve an Karen how ter rob the casino wid no comebacks, I sez.

—No fuckin comebacks, he sez, —half of the Greater Manchester Police force are huntin them. The Yorkshire Ripper'll be out before that pair. That's if they decide ter take them an whoever is wid them alive an don't shoot ter fuckin kill.

—I dint mean it ter come ter this, I sez.

—Drunk, he sez, —you're goin down. Proper time.

—No, yer don't understand, I sez, —I aint done nothin. I wasn't even there for any of it.

Silence.

—Wot should I do? I ask.

—Fuck knows, sez Macca, —see Doctor Singh an get yerself signed inter Parkhouse.

—There's fuck all wrong wid me, I sez.

—Tell that Billy Kelly's family, he sez, —tell that ter Maurice's kids. It IS you, it aint that tosser, Steve, he aint got the fuckin brains. How many more?

—Look, I sez, —can I come to yours an have a drink?

Another silence.

—No, he sez.

An it's the first time he's ever let me down.

—Right, I sez, —look after yerself an look after Serenity an the kids.

—Drunk, he sez, —don't go near Steve or Karen. Understand? Stay clear.

—Yeah, I sez an I hang up.

An a feel gutted. The chickens are comin home ter roost.

Steve and Karen leave Billy's flat, with the door ajar for no other reason than indifference. They head for an old people's bungalow that Steve has done work on during his Community Service stint. They get in and make themselves comfortable.

—'Mama I just killed a man', sings Steve.

—It's all right here, says Kaz, —how long can we stay for?

—Till Mrs Jarvis comes home, says Steve.

—When's that Babs? asks Karen.

—Friday, says Steve.

—Well why dint yer just say fuckin Friday then? snaps Karen.

Steve is impervious.

—Sorted here, he says. —Community Service has its benefits. Look at them winda locks, Kaz, no fucker could break in here.

—We just did, points out Karen.

—Yeah, but I had a key, says Steve, smiling.

He goes in a cabinet under the telly and comes out with a bottle of Taylor's, and him and Karen enjoy a Port and lemon. —This, he says, —is the dog's gonads. He pulls Karen to the floor, —I'm pinin for Grimsby, he says, tugging on her knickers.

I'm sat in me flat readin last night's *Evenin News*. The news of the day is Steve an Karen. There's a lovely picture of em taken on holiday in Benidorm. Karen's wearin a turquoise bikini that make her nipples stand out. She's smilin serenely at the camera, whilst Steve stands grinnin wid one hand stuck down his trunks. There's another story about an unnamed man bein arrested at a lock-up in Hendham Vale. And an interview wid Detective Inspector Mulcahy who calls us, 'A dangerous group of people with underworld connections'. Apparently arrests are imminent.

I look at the clock. It's eleven. I go ter the kitchen an brew up. The milk smells sour. I end up havin a black coffee stood at the winda. As the traffic staggers around the roads below, I think about what'll happen if it all comes on top. About me mam, an how she'll cope wid the neighbours. About me brother in Cambridge, how he'll be dragged into it all. An how me kids'll be pointed out in the street.

I think of me dad. He never stole in his life. I see his face before me, an I can't face him. He died on this Avenue I'm looking down at, me dad, killed by a hit an run. He grafted for forty year, dug drains, ditches sewers an roads. Fought in a World War. He was never unemployed an never joined a Union. 'Never had to,' he used ter say, an point to his hands. He told great stories about when he was on the lump in Leeds. About comin home on trains an how he'd buy a book of raffle tickets, then raffle his wages, an all the other mad navvies, brickies an wotever ud buy a ticket. Told me about Ginley's shite. One day old Ginley an me dad were out diggin an Ginley needed a shite. So he nips behind this bush, drops his strides an goes about his business. In the meantime, me dad sticks his shovel under the bush unbeknownst ter Ginley. An Ginley shit's on the shovel an me dad pulls it away. Anyway, a minute later all yer hear is this howl an Ginley comes tearin around the bush shoutin, 'Seanie, I know I had a shit but can I fuck find it!'

At seventy he was still workin on site as a navvy. There's no sentiment on site, if yer can't hack it you're out. Me old man could still hack it. Then one August night he's walkin home from the pub, half pissed, but what's that matter, he paid for his own fuckin beer, an he gets hit by a car. It splattered him all over Victoria Avenue.

A doctor was one of the first on the scene an said me dad died instantly. So no sufferin. Aye maybe not for him. I got ter find out early the next mornin. I was livin wid Debbie in Newton Heath when it happened, in our first little house (the one that got repossessed when *The Fellow* got photo-finished at Cheltenham). We only had the one kid, little Brendan, an he was about three month old at the time.

Anyway at about two in the mornin there's a load of hammerin on me front door. I get up, look out the winda an I see a couple of police wid me brother, Eammon. An unusual mix, I'm thinkin, cos he never gets in trouble, he's not the sort. So I figure he's got pissed an given my address. So I dress, go downstairs, an open the door.

As I do so our Eammon sez, —I'll only be five minutes, Officers.

An the police go back to their car.

It's weird, he's tellin them what ter do. Aint he read the script? I think any minute now he turns inter George Best, cos this is a fuckin dream.

—Take as long as you want, sez one of the police.

Me head's still tryin ter get round what's happenin. Eammon walks in, I follow him through. Debbie comes downstairs carryin Brendan, the commotion's woken him up.

—Eammon looks at me an sez, —Me dad's dead.

I've bin punched hard, but I don't wanna fall.

—How? I sez.

—Run over. I've just bin ter identify him.

—Right, I sez.

When we were kids me dad taught us that you're only beat when you admit you're beat. If you laugh in their faces, no matter what the scoreboard of life sez, then you aint beat. If they've got you pinned down an you're battered an you're bleedin, spit at em. But don't ever give in.

I don't know what ter say. Eammon looks at me, motions at the door an sez, —Gotta go. Me mam's on her own wid the dogs. She'll wanna know what's happened.

I nod at him an he leaves.

I look over at Debbie. She's cryin. She's holdin Brendan an he's cryin. I aint cryin. I notice there's a chocolate stain on the new carrycot. I point to the stain an scream at her. —Look at that, yer scruffy bitch! Do yer think I'm takin me baby out in that? Hey? You mighta bin dragged up, but I fuckin wasn't. This whole house is a pigsty! I'm shoutin, an I'm screamin an I'm cryin. It's funny, I never knew I loved me dad till he died. I'm just sat there, I can't move. It's the early hours. Debbie starts cleanin the carrycot an gettin the baby ready.

—What yer doin? I sez.

—We better get to yer mam's. She'll need yer, she sez.

I get dressed in a haze. The phone had bin cut off at the time so we had ter push the baby to the other side of Brookdale Park. It's a wild night. As we pass the Horseshoe pub we step inter the road to avoid a fallen tree. I have visions of me dad doin the same, an walkin under a car. I'm angry at the old man an there's nothin I can do about it, but cry. Me an Debbie are walkin, wordless. Debbie phones a taxi an we wait at the call box for it. I can't remember if it come right away or if it took an hour. When it arrives the driver's one of them mouthy fuckers. Normally I can give as good as I get, but fuck, I don't need this now. Debs tries ter shut him up by sayin we've just lost someone close, but he don't wanna hear, he just keeps on about someone he's took ter Clayton who won't pay the fare. I get annoyed an sez, —Yeah, someone just made a jigsaw outta me dad.

We're dropped off in silence outside of me mam's.

All the lights are on, so I just tap on the winda. Eammon answers it. We follow him in. I put the baby on the couch. Me mam offers me a cup of tea but I need somethin a bit stronger, so Eammon pours me a whisky. We all sit there in silence like we're a group of strangers waitin for the same bus, but I have ter get it over with.

—What happened? I sez.

Eammon takes me inter the other room an we sit down. He starts talkin. As he's talkin, he's starin at an electric fire that aint on:

—He was late comin home. We thought we'd give it a while. You know how he is if he gets talkin. It gets on a bit, so me mam starts ter get a bit worried. She sez she's goin ter the bottom of the street. So I sez, 'take the dogs wid yer, if there's anyone hangin about

166

the dogs'll see em off'. She's gone twenty minutes an when she gets back she's got a copper wid her. 'What's up?' I sez.

I shuffle an sigh as Eammon continues:

—Then she tells me that when she got ter the bottom of the street the police were puttin up cordons. There's no one about that she knows. So she goes over an gives a young copper me dad's description. The young copper has a word wid a Sergeant an then he brings me mam home. He aint told her nothin yet. He asks her ter sit down. He asks who I am, an I tell him. Then he tells us it's a hit an run an that me dad's dead. He sez that he died instantly. Made it sound just like coffee. It's not fair that, ter be honest, I felt sorry for him, not much of a job is it? He tells us that he'll get the bastard. Then he apologises for swearin. I'm thinkin that unless when they get him he's carryin magic Sellotape that'll put me dad back tergether, there's not much point. I don't even wanna know his name. Then they took me ter identify him in some place at the back of the Daily Express. I go in, an they show me his body. I was hopin it was all a big mistake. I was hopin it was someone else but it wasn't, it was Dad. He looked all right. He didn't look bruised or anythin. He looked just like he always looked. I thanked the Officer. He asks me ter sign a form an then they took me to your house.

Eammon finishes talkin. He hasn't looked up once. I'm stunned.

—I owe him nine quid, I sez.

It seems daft, but that's all that come into me head.

An that's it, me dad parcelled inter the past along wid Beethoven, Elvis an Nat King Cole. Forty continuous years on site, a war veteran an it all ends age seventy walkin home from a pub. An when me marriage ended, I got a flat on the Avenue where he died. An there aint a single day that goes by that I don't think of him. Now here I am. An I can't look me dad's ghost in the face.

I finish me coffee, still tryin ter analyse the position I'm in. The plan seems ter have taken on a life of it's own. How was I supposed ter budget for a winda cleana gettin socked an Durie gettin dragged inter it? It's that butterfly's wings. Someone wants ter get that butterfly an rip it's fuckin wings off. Everythin's driftin beyond my control. On the plus side, it's two days on an the police have shown no interest in me. The only direct connection they could make with me an the crime is through Karen an Steve. So I've gotta see Strange an Crazy tomorrow an convince em that they gotta get abroad. Then if I keep me head down I'm in the clear. If they stay loose an the police go door ter door someone might just mention me. But if anyone was gonna grass that knew anythin worth knowin they'd of done it by now. Thank fuck there aint no reward.

I continue chewin through all the scenarios.

Karen is channel hopping, watching the news to see herself and Steve. She's already got a good forty-five minutes recorded on a video cassette she's borrowed off Mrs Jarvis.

—What's 'heinous' mean, Babs? asks Karen.

—Horrible an nasty, says Steve.

—Bastards, says Karen, —they don't even know us. I worked in a care home once.

—LOOK, shouts Steve, —the Global Casino's offerin a twenty grand reward for us!

—Each or together? asks Kaz.

—Tergether Babs, says Steve.

—Still ten grand aint bad, says Kaz.

—Wunt it be great, says Steve, —if they post Wanted posters all over?

—Fuckin mint, says Kaz, —I'd have ter have one a them for me bedroom wall.

—I told yer I'd make it a little bit like the movies for yer, says Steve. —Right, he adds, —we're down ter our last bullet. I shouldn't have wasted that one on the pigeon.

—I bet the pigeon was thinkin that too, says Karen, —an if we have a suicide pact you go first.

Steve laughs. —We need some drink, he says, — got any money?

—A fuckin bag full, says Karen, laughing.

—I gotta ease up on the stuff, says Steve, —me heads like a council flat in Hulme.

—We'll have to toss for who's goin for the carry out, both our pictures have bin on telly an in the papers, says Karen.

—No problemo, says Steve, an fishes out a coin.

—Tails never fails, shouts Karen.

Karen puts a long leather on, a pair of glasses and a scarf, and goes to the Chinese off licence.

While she's out, Steve plans a surprise. He strips naked and ties a yellow ribbon round his dick.

At the off licence, Karen gets a couple of bottles of vodka, some mixers, and four packets of quavers.

Outside, a few lads try and enter into banter.

—Fuck me, says one, motioning towards Karen's coat, —it's Cruella DeVille.

Karen walks on unperturbed. She's never seen *One Hundred And One Dalmatians* so she thinks it's just a case of mistaken identity.

Meanwhile, back at the pensioner's bungalow, Steve is hid in the cloakroom, ready to leap out and surprise his baby. Five minutes go by and he hears the key in the door. The door shuts. He gives Karen ten seconds to turn round and he leaps out, bollock naked, ribbon on his dick and waving two feather dusters.

Mrs Jarvis screams and faints.

Karen returns from the off licence just in time to help carry Mrs Jarvis onto the couch.

—Aw bless, says Karen, —she's out like a light.

I wake up Wednesday an I'm bouncin: another day passed an no knock in the night. I aint slept proper for three days, but each day brings wid it a little more hope. I decide ter get some beans an toast down me. I flick the telly on an no news is good news. Other stories are breakin an Steve an Karen have bin relegated to a ten second slot on the local reports. I don't have ter ring Strange an Crazy till four, so I shave a shower an have a bit of a sing song while I'm about it.

It suddenly hits me, I don't love Debbie anymore. It's all gone. There's nothin like an armed robbery an a bit of murder ter help yer through lovesickness. I decide this is the turnin point, this is the first day of the rest of my life. An I'm gonna fuckin well enjoy it.

I catch a 123 down Rochdale Road ter the Crown an Anchor. As I get there, a crowd of fuckin office workers are goin in. Twenty minutes of queuein later, I take me two pints of bitter change an go sit in the corner ter mind me own buisness. An who should come an plonk his self next ter me but Carl.

—This seat taken? he sez, laffin.

I smile. He's great company Carl, a compulsive gambler.

—What yer up to? I ask.

—Fuck all, he sez, —just havin a mooch round town.

—Done owt lately? I sez (meanin, has Dame Fortune smiled on you in the bookmakers since we

170

last chatted?).

Have I fuck, he sez, —yesterday I broke even. I needed to as well cos it was me gas money an I bin cut off four times. Have yer seen them new elecky meters?

—No, I sez, confused.

—They call em goldfish bowls, he continues, —yer can't fiddle em. They're about as big as yer average rat trap. Did I tell yer why they give it me?

—Yer won a surprise draw, I suggest.

—Naw kidder, he continues laffin at his own story, —I had it runnin back. Right? So wot I do is run it back for a month, run it forward for a month an then pay for a month. But I like a drop of cider an I forget, an I'm always out when they come. They send me a bailiff's or whatever for entry, so I put me meter right. But there's no seals on it, so I see me mate Johnny an he gives me some, so it looks the part.

—Pint? I sez, not waitin for is answer, an head for the bar. While I'm there I think, fuck it, an get two gin an tonics in as well.

—Here, I sez, when I'm back with Carl, —drink this.

Cheers, sez Carl. —Where was I?

—Awaitin a visit from the elecky, I sez.

—Yeah, so the elecky come an I let em in. An this great big fella sez 'I'm not happy wid the seals', so I sez back, 'What fuckin seals? We're not allowed pets in these flats.'

I fall about laffin.

—An they put this goldfish bowl over me meter, he finishes, —an they drill it ter the wall. An big bollocks tells me it's 'tamper proof'. An I sez, 'Yeah well why've yer drilled it ter the wall then?' That got him thinkin. You out all day?

—No, I sez, —business in Plattin.

—Fuckin hell, he sez, —it's not the same round there anymore. Everytime yer turn on the news there's another one bin shot. You workin?

—Not this week, I sez, —I'm on holiday.

—Where yer graftin? he asks.

—I'm on a Reception at a casino, I sez.

—No shit, he sez, a little too excited.

—Which one?

—The Global, I sez.

—Do yer know a manager there called Bella? he asks.

Me blood runs cold.

—Yeah, I sez.

—Yer won't believe this, sez Carl, —but last Sunday I'm in the flat mindin me own business. I look out the winda at the playin fields, hopin ter see a bit of crumpet, an what do I see?

I shrug.

—Only this women wid her skirt up her arse who I think has bin stood up. So I gives it twenty minutes an still no show. By this time she's clocked me, so I wave, but she looks the other way. So I think fuck it. I get another bottle of Strongbow down me, an decide I might as well go down, an try me luck. So I make up a little picnic, nothin much, some cider, a box of After Eights an a couple a dinky pork pies. I think we can sit on the grassy knoll there an have a laugh. But I gets down there an the next thing yer know she's cryin. So I thinks, here's me chance, an I take her up to me flat. All the way up in the lift she's cryin an I'm hopin she aint noticed the smell of the piss. When we get in the flat she asks can she use the phone. 'Yeah' I sez. An guess who she fuckin rang.

—The police, I sez.

—How'd yer know? he sez, puzzled.

—A work at the casino, I sez, —what yer think of

172

her?

—Good lookin woman for her age, he sez.

An I'm thinkin outrageous coincidences like this only happen in books. Either way, I think, better ter get away from Carl.

I down me pint an sez, —just nippin ter the toilet.

An I fuck off up ter the Kings. I need peace an quiet, so I sit in their beer garden. It's a converted outside toilet, with high walls ter three sides. It's got a bench set slung in the middle. Agoraphobiacs catch more sun than yer could catch in that garden, but I can get a little peace an get me head tergether widout hearin about dead winda cleanas an kidnapped manageresses. I decide ter get me moby out an ring the casino to find out what's goin on.

Colin picks up.

—Hello Global Casino. Colin speakin. How can I help you?

—Well modulated tones, I sez, —just like in the manual. I'll have ter tell Jeanette ter get yer a Karma Sutra an see if yer can stick ter that as well.

—Drunk, he whispers, —I'll ring yer back on yer mobby. Give us a minute.

An I get panicky. What the fuck's goin on?

I go ter take a swig of me pint an me moby goes off. The beer goes everywhere. Me nerves are shot ter fuck. Good job there's no one watchin cos they'd think I was doin the sign of the cross wid the thing.

I take Colin's call.

—Don't know what's happenin Drunk, he sez, —but your name keeps croppin up.

—How? I sez.

—Shifts yer worked, he sez, —an shifts yer didn't work.

—Right, I sez, —don't tell no fucker that I rang.

—Yer don't have ter tell me that mate, he sez, —an

good luck.

It's obvious he knows I done it, but his loyalty brings a lump ter me throat.

—See yer Colin, I sez.

I look at me watch. It's three thirty. Half an hour ter go till I can ring me comrades. I order another pint an go for a piss. I kill a bit of time by readin the graffiti.

There's a poem by someone called Barry Newroad:

Just like the Marie Celeste
no one else was there
not a swingin lightbulb
not a rockin chair
it was the suicide bombers reunion
an no one else was there.

I read it two or three times, an I like it. It sez it all about the futility of patriotism. An who really gives a fuck? The Americans? The biggest killer in the world terday is dirty water. Yet the Americans declare war on Terrorism. Why don't they spend a few fuckin quid on cleanin the water? Why don't they give a thousand million shillins ter Uganda in the hope that some nine year old kids get ter see a bit a life?

I realise I must be gettin fairly drunk ter be so worked up, or it's the lack of sleep. I daren't sleep cos I know I'd see Billy an Maurice an Sheila Grimes, an me dad turning away, an a hundred other things in me dreams that I'd pay not ter see.

Simple As

Steve and Karen lay out Mrs Jarvis on the couch. Karen has taken a shine to her. She's gone off the idea of having a dog. Now she wants a Nana. Half-an-hour later, Mrs Jarvis wakes and Karen finds out that the grey haired sweet old lady who she's adopted as a surrogate Nana is in fact a foul mouthed, barking mad old bat.

—Who the fuck are you? shouts Mrs Jarvis at Karen, —yer anorexic little fuckin bitch.

—Calm down, says Karen.

—Calm fuckin down? repeats Mrs J, —I'd wring your neck like a twattin chicken if I wasn't tied down.

Karen goes over to her.

—Don't come near me, yer prostitute, says Mrs J, —where's that long streak a piss gone? Showin a pensioner his John Thomas. Me husband's was twice as big an fuckin thicker.

—Shush Nana, says Karen.

—Fuckin Nana, yells Mrs J, —I'll give yer Nana. Do yer think I coulda bred a fuck, fuckin, twat like you?

An it goes on an on like an obscene train. All you can hear is 'fuckety-fuck, fuckety-fuck, fuckety-fuckety-fuck'.

—Shut it Edna, says Steve, —we're expecting a phone call.

—Fuck yer fuckin phone call, says Edna, —I'm gonna tell the fuckin probation about you. A bet this is in fuckin breach of it. No ski-in in Switzerland for you, yer fuckin cunt.

—Karen, says Steve, —put a sock in her gob.

So Karen goes to the linen basket and gets a pair of tights, rolls them into a little ball, and stuffs them in Edna's gob. She gets some Sellotape and runs it round three or four times.

—Breathe through yer nose, says Karen.

—Awwww, says Steve, —the sounds of silence.

—God, what an handful, says Karen.

And Steve tells Karen the history of Mrs Edna Jarvis, while Edna sits there, fuming and snorting along.

—She's the eldest Turret's Syndrome sufferer in England. She's had it since she was a kid. Bin in homes an looney bins, they thought she was a lettuce short of a salad.

—Still, says Karen, —a time an a place for everythin.

—No, says Steve, —yer don't understand, she don't know she's swearin. Honest.

—She must, says Kaz, —it's her doin it.

—No, it's involuntary, says Steve, —she don't get a say in it.

—Oh, says Kaz, —like me wid our lottery numbers?

—The other week, says Steve steering clear of the lottery subject, —she was talkin to the priest an she said, 'God be fuckin wid yer Father, yer cunt'. No, she's a very famous Mancunian, aint yer Edna? They've done supplements in papers an she's bin on a World in Action. This woman is an iconoclast.

Steve's off, discussing the treatment Edna must have received in the loony bin.

—They'd a fired electric through her, cut bits of her brain out an no doubt the male nurses gang-banged her. It all went on, yer know.

The phone rings.

Steve picks up. It's the Drunk.

—Steve, you there?

—'I won't let a Nun go down on me', Steve sings.

—Right Steve, wot do yer want? says the Drunk over the phone.

—Ter give you yer money, Steve says, —an then

it's bye-bye.

—Right, lets meet on the Railway car park, says the Drunk.

—No fuckin way, Steve says, —me an Kaz are wanted. Every fucker's lookin for us.

—Where then?

—What about here? Steve says.

—Where the fuck's here?

—You not taped up are yer? Steve says.

—Taped up? What the fuck you on about? says the Drunk.

—This aint bein recorded is it? Steve says, and he's tense.

—Not at this fuckin end, the Drunk says.

Steve gives the Drunk directions and tells him to wait in a back entry, he'll meet him there at six. He hangs up.

Steve and Karen take a quiet spliff.

—Let's give Nana a breather, says Karen, an she unrolls the Sellotape.

—Now no swearin, says Kaz, an sits down.

Edna shakes herself to her senses.

—Mumfly fuckin crumfly fuck cunts, she says.

—Her old self, says Steve.

—What I don't understand, says Karen, —is how yer know?

—How yer know what, Babs? says Steve.

—How yer know when she's genuinely tellin yer ter fuck off or when it's like she's just got her illness?

—I know, says Steve, —it must be fuckin frustratin.

—Yeah, says Karen drawing deep on her cig, —like a dog wid no tail that can't let other dogs know if she's friendly or not.

—FUCKIN WHORES MELTS YER CUNTS, shouts Edna.

Steve grabs the Sellotape and then he grabs Edna's

head. The roll of Sellotape goes one way and her head goes the other. There's a noise like ten knuckles cracking simultaneously, and Karen is Nanaless once again. Steve checks. He's broken Edna's neck.

—What do we do? says Karen.

—Bung her in the kitchen, Steve says, —I've gotta meet Drunk in a minute. An yer know wot a fuckin whinger he is.

So they sit Edna in her favourite chair in the kitchen, then go back into the living room.

—This is gettin every night, says Karen.

—Fuckin hell, says Steve, —I couldn't let her talk to yer like that.

Steve goes out to meet the Drunk.

I put the phone down. I realise I've got two hours ter kill before I meet Steve and Kaz, an nowhere ter go. Then I remember Kathy. She lives above an off licence in Ancoats an likes ter party so she's usually up for a drink. I head there. When I get there I have ter knock her up.

—Fuckin hell, I sez, —gone four an yer still in bed.

—Late night, she sez, —nip downstairs an get a bottle of vodka.

So I go inter the shop an get a bottle of vodka an a bottle of coke.

—For Kathy? the Greek lad sez.

—Yeah, I sez.

—You tell her ter pay her rent, he sez, —or you pay it for her, maybe?

—Maybe not, I sez, an head back upstairs.

I get sat down an I'm weighin Kathy up. Not bad for a women of her age. A couple of vodkas down me an I might chance it.

—Do yer wanna see what the kids' dad's got the

kids? she asks.

I don't really but I sez yeah, an she fucks off in the kitchen.

She comes out wid about twenty kids' outfits.

—Yeah, sorted, I sez, —gotta be a couple of ton's worth there.

—Third lot this month, she sez.

—I gotta give the man his due, I sez, —he looks after them kids. What's he do for a livin?

—He's a shoplifter, she sez, —an yer never go short when yer a lifter.

She sez it as if it's a trade akin ter plumbin or joinery.

—Sling a tape on, I sez.

She puts some sorta shite on.

—Who the fuck's this? I ask.

—Dunno, she sez, — it's one of Naomi's. She's inter all this moody stuff.

I pour us another vodka an ask her what's happenin in her life. There aint a lot. I'm two parts drunk now, an she's startin ter look desirable. I mooch on over ter the couch, but she don't want no go, so I leave it. I look at me watch. I've killed an hour. I bung Kathy a tenner, say, —see yer when I see yer, then jump a 163 ter Harpurhey.

I walk through from the Harpurhey Hip side of the estate, so I can see where I'm goin before I get there. I'm worried about traps an police but I'm more worried that Steve might blame me for what's happenin an shoot me.

I get ter the entry an I'm there at the time arranged. I'm opposite a pub called the Jolly Carter an wonderin if the barmy bastard is in there half-pissed. I pace up and down a bit. Where the fuck is he? I decide ter give him ten minutes, an then if he aint here I'll peer through the pub winda, an if he aint there then fuck knows wot. There's a bit of a chill in the air an I can

feel it in me bones. I blow warm air on me hands. —
Where the fuck is he?

A spin round in fear but there's nobody there. God,
I'm crackin up.

I hear a noise from the other side of the road so I
lean back behind a wheelie bin. A couple of teenagers
exit the Jolly. It seems ter be workin for them, cos
they look positively giddy as they head down towards
the Ark Royal. I watch them till they're outta me sight
an a think ter meself, yer can always tell an
impoverished area, the pubs are fuckin hammered all
day.

I start goin through what I'm gonna tell Steve. I
gotta be in full control an keep him in control of hisself.
An I gotta detach meself from Karen for good. I hear
another noise an I nearly jump outta me skin. There's
a dog growlin at me. Some woman appears an sez,
—What yer doin lurkin there?

—Nothin, I sez.

—Well yer look like yer lurkin ter me, she sez, —an
I'm Neighbourhood Watch.

I'm thinkin, what the fuck is this? —Look, Missus,
I sez in a pleasant voice, —I'm waitin for me mate. I
can't go to his house cos his wife don't like me.

—I'm keepin me eye on you, she sez, —an don't be
surprised if I don't ring our local Bobby.

I decide ter fuck off but just as I do, Steve comes
round the corner.

—See luv, I sez ter the old girl, —not everybody's a
burglar.

I walk over ter Steve an shake his hand.

—Get a drink in, sez Steve, handin me sixty quid.

—A bit much here, I sez.

—It's out of your share, laughs Steve, —an get a
bottle of champagne.

I get a bottle of Moet et Chandon, twelve cans a

Stella, a bottle of gin an a bottle of tonic water. We walk ter the bungalow.

—Everythin okay? I ask.

—Don't worry, Drunk, he sez, —we aint settin yer up ter kill yer for your share. We already got it, remember?

We get back ter Mrs Jarvis's. It's in the dark. Steve knocks on the winda an Karen answers it.

—Guess who's comin ter dinner? sez Steve.

We walk past Karen an inter the bungalow. As we're walkin in, Karen, who's followin behind me, feels me arse. Me nerves are so shot that it completely boo's me head.

—Argh! I let out.

—Wot the fucks wrong wid yer? sez Steve, turnin.

—Indigestion, I sez.

—Fuck sakes, Drunk, he sez, —calm down.

We go in the livin room. They've got the money split up inter three bundles.

—That's your one, sez Kaz pointin ter the nearest one, —it's two grand light.

Typical, I'm thinkin, they murder Billy an pocket his share. But I aint in the mood for arguin. —I need a drink, I sez, grabbin the bottle of vodka, —where's the glasses?

—In the kitchen, sez Karen, sniggerin.

I head ter the kitchen. I enter an I stop in me tracks. There's a body wid a Sainsbury's bag over its head perched up on a chair.

—Holy Mary Mother of God! I shout an come runnin back in ter the livin room to a laffin Steve an Karen.

I'm shakin like a leaf, an I'm cryin. It's finally all got ter me. I've seen a dead body an this aint an episode of *The Bill*, It's real fuckin life. I'm scared shitless. They might murder me next. I sit on a threadbare chair an me mouth's open an I'm pantin like a greyhound after a race. Me eyes are spaced out. I can't get me thoughts ter run consecutive.

—Fuccccccccckkkkkkkkk, I sez through closed teeth.

—Soun's just like Edna, sez Karen.

—Who've yer killed? I sez, —an why?

I'm shakin. I'm tryin ter pour a vodka an it's goin all over.

—Just followin instructions, sez Steve, smilin.

—Whose fuckin instructions? I sez, gulpin raw vodka.

—Yours of course, sez Steve.

—Remember in that nursin home, he sez, — remember what yer said about frogs?

—Noooo, I sez, teeth chatterin wid fear.

—Yer said that in a frog pond when there aint enough food for all the frogs, that all the young frogs jump on the old frogs backs an choke the old ones ter death. Yer said it was nature, 'Old frogs first' yer said.

I look at him.

—But what had she done? I sez.

—Drunk, let's not fall out about this, he sez, —but I just did what I was told.

I'm sat there like a cornered rabbit, listenin.

—Right, he sez, —me an Kaz are gonna take our chances an head for Hull. So this is where we end it all.

The gun wid the one bullet is on the table. I'm weighin up smackin him wid the vodka bottle an shootin him. Then I realise I don't know how ter work the gun. An if he's got the safety catch thingy on it, an if it don't shoot when I pull the trigger, then he'll strangle me as sure as eggs is an anagram of fuck all. I lose me moment an sit back. I gotta get out of here soon or not at all.

—Here, he sez, —your share.

He passes me an Aldi bag full of money. I don't want it.

—I don't want it, I sez.

There's a dead silence.

—Look, he sez, —I had this out wid Billy Kelly. Rather you take it mate or I make yer a paper fuckin shroud out of it.

—ENOUGH, shouts Kaz, —I aint havin yer talk ter the Drunk like that. Have some respect.

An it's madness, total unadulterated madness.

—Look, I sez, —you an Kaz are wanted an that an I'm in the clear. Call my share inconvenience money. Yer've earned it an yer need it. Take it an when things settle down, send for me. Yer could invest it, an when I get there, yer coulda bought me a bar. 'Drunks Bar'.

Steve sits down.

—We fuckin did it though, dint we? he sez, an his smile lights up the room, —a bunch of Miles Plattin nobodies, but we had over a fuckin casino, dint we?

He's right an I feel a sense a pride. Karen gets out the bottle of champagne an we do a toast.

—Casinos, I've fuckin shit the cunts, sez Steve the toast master.

—Casinos we've fuckin shit the cunts, sez me an Karen in reply.

We have this drink tergether an Steve explains his theory.

—It's me genes, he sez.

I stare at his jeans.

—No, me genes, he sez, —me biological make up.

—What yer on about? I sez.

—I got killin genes, he sez, —musta inherited 'em off me dad. He used ter hunt rabbits.

—Yeah? I sez.

—An you Drunk, yer got drinkin genes, he sez, —an yer dad was a drunk.

—An I got shaggin genes, sez Kaz, —got em off me mam.

—So that's the solution, he sez, —yer mix killin genes wid shaggin an drinkin genes an yer got murder an stuff.

I think about what he's just said an it makes sense. Nobody really planned nothin, it was in our genes from the start. I laff an start to sing,

'That's the way God planned it'.

'The Gene Genie loves chimney stacks', sings Steve.

An then he cuts off complete an sez,

—Ever heard that song, *Poetry In Motion*? There's a line in that, that's fuckin brilliant.

—Which one? I sez.

An he sings,

'She's much too nice to re-arrrrrrrrange'.

An I'm laffin, I can see where he's goin.

—He's sliced up all his ex girlfriend's, Steve sez, — an this one better watch out.

I laff an wonder if he's bein allegoric.

We have another drink tergether an I decide ter go while everythin's still sorted.

—Right, I sez, —I'm off.

An it's quite tearful in a hushed sorta way. We say goodbye in a back entry.

—Good luck, I sez.

—You too, Drunk, sez Karen an kisses me.

—I've killed for less, sez Steve, huggin me.

An Steve stands in dog shit.

—Ter fuck an back, he shouts.

—It's good luck, sez Karen.

As I walk back towards the Oldham Road I find meself laffin. I'm not sure wot about, but I like it. It's the old me, back like what I was like before the divorce an everythin. I aint gettin told by strangers on buses that I'm cryin no more. Okay, it's mad what we done.

But I don't care, cos even if I go ter prison, it's fuckin better than starin at a wall cryin.

Steve and Karen pack up their things and start to make plans.

—What we gonna do? Karen says.

—Head for Hull, Steve says.

—Yer know anyone there? asks Karen.

—No, he says picking up the bag of money, —don't need to know people. All the knowin in the world's in this bag.

—How are we gonna get there? she says.

—Charlie Marley, says Steve.

—Oh no, says Kaz, —he's fuckin up it.

—We aint got a choice, says Steve, —an if we have, everythin's got spam in it.

Steve gets on the moby and phones his old cell mate from Detention Centre, Recalls, Remand, YP, and proper nick.

—Charlie it's me, Steve.

Karen listens. She can only hear Steve's part:

—Yeah a bit of bother, says Steve.............Naw fuck...........Yeah......Need yer man.....Old team an that back tergether...... You got transport?.. ... Wot yer got?..... Yeah......Snooker ball in a sock....Yeah snatched from us like a pregnant woman's handbag on Newton Heath market..... 'Splish splash I was takin a bath'....No..........Yeah.......Coool........Remember that goat?.....Hehehehehe........Need yer tomorra ......Bring yer bird.....Make a day of it.....Wot?.......Twelve outside May's pawn shop......Okay?.......Yeah?......An thanks mate......There's   ten   grand   in   it   for yer.....Haha......Catch yer later flatulater.

Steve hangs up. He's buoyant. —Charlie'll know people in Hull, he says, —he did a four stretch in there.

—He'll know Screws, says Karen, —that's all he'll know, an fuckin convicts.

I finally get me 82 an head down ter Miles Plattin. I check me pockets. I've got about forty eight quid. Fuck it, I think, I'll head for Rentadad's. I get off the bus an hit the offy. As usual there's a group of teenage knobheads congregatin outside waitin ter start somethin. I barge past em sayin, —Gangway, payin customer comin through. Soup kitchen open at Nine.

They sneer back their juvenile replies, but I'm past em an in the shop before they realise what's happenin.

I pick up four Stellas from the fridge an head for the counter.

I survey the motley array of spirits available an order a bottle of Gorky vodka an a bottle of tonic water. I pay for me drink an walk outside. I'm met by a deposition.

A kid about fourteen sez, —you said our Damon had big ears.

—Did he pay me for the consultation? I sez, tryin ter walk round him, —tell him ter pin his ears back an wait for me bill.

I walk on an, THUMP, somethin smacks me in me back. I get jumped an kicked. I'm down on the floor, next door ter the chippy. I take a good kick ter the head. Me glasses go flyin off. I get me hand stood on. I know I gotta get up or die.

—Who's got big ears now? shouts fourteen.

I spit blood an think of me dad.

—The Mafia have cos Noddy won't pay the ransom. Another kick, an another kick.

I wake up in the chippy on a bench. Some concerned meddlin bastard is about ter ring an ambulance.

—No, I sez, —leave it, I'm okay.

I struggle ter me feet, thinkin ter meself, thank fuck his mates dint join in.

Me glasses are bent an buckled, me bottle of vodka's broke an they've made off wid me cans.

I hobble round ter Renta's.

When I get there, the door's on the latch, so I go in an close the door behind me.

—Renta! I shout. He comes wanderin out inter the hall.

—Fuck, he sez, —wot happened ter you?

—A misunderstandin, I sez. He helps me inter the livin room.

There's some old girl sat on the couch wid a top too low an a skirt too high. She reminds me of one of these fellas in their fifties who still play Sunday league football. Don't they know they're past it?

—Oooh Jesus, she sez when she sees me, —I'm off.

—No wait, Mavis, Renta sez.

—No chance, sez Mavis, —I can't stand blood. Me own periods used ter be a trauma, I can tell yer, a daredn't look down.

Mavis pulls her skirt into a more respectable position an leaves us to it.

—Fuckin hell, sez Renta, —I was on for a fuck there.

—Got any drink? I ask.

—Pernod, he sez, —I got it for her.

—Wot yer wanna fuck *her* for? I sez.

—She's me landlady, he sez.

—Oh, I sez an change the subject. —You an Rafferty made up yet?

—No fuckin chance, he sez, an I can tell he's lost widout him.

I swill back me Pernod an lime.

—Wot yer gonna do? he sez.

—About wot? I ask.

—You're in a load a shit, he sez.

—Why? I sez, wonderin wot he's talkin about.

—Drunk, he sez, —you an Crazy Steve an Karen an Billy robbed the Global. Simple as. Since then them two have bin murderin people. I think you're on their list. I reckon their workin backwards an you're number one.

At this point he mimes a gun firin.

—How'd yer know all this? I ask.

—Who fuckin doesn't? he replies.

I sit there battered, bewildered an buggered.

—Every fucker knows?

—Just about, he sez, —an even the police must know by now. That fuckin cleana in the Housin will a told her son, an he's a copper.

—Yeah I've met him, I sez, gulpin the Pernod down.

—So wot yer gonna do? he asks.

I shrug me shoulders. —Get drunk wid you. Get a taxi home an wait for em.

—Get a Brief first, he sez.

—No point, I sez.

An we sit back an watch the telly. I'm half-pissed an noddin so I head for the toilet. I find meself pissin blood. *Claret on tap*, I think. I wash me hands, givin the rusty lookin bar of soap a miss an look round the bathroom for somethin ter dry them on. There's nothin that wouldn't dirty em more. I decide, for health an safety reasons, ter wipe me hands on me jeans.

When I come back Renta's got *Crimewatch* on the box. There's three pictures on the telly. Steve, Karen an me. The one of me was taken on a casino outin ter Blackpool an it looks like I'm cryin on it. Considerin it was taken the week after the divorce settlement, I probably was.

He turns the sound up. It's Detective Inspector George Mulcahy.

—...also known as the Drunk. He may be travellin with Reilly an Tucker or he may be travellin independently.

What a shit sentence, I'm thinkin, I mean it's gotta be one or he other, aint it?

They cut the camera back ter George.

—*These people are extremely dangerous and should be approached with care. Anyone helping with information leading to the apprehendin of any of the three will receive a twenty thousand pounds reward.*

Fuckin dangerous? I've just bin beat up by a fourteen year old, I'm about as dangerous as a wounded butterfly. George then goes on to link everythin that had happened to organised crime in the Chinese community.

I sit stunned. Me mam will of watched that an will be in hysterics. They've no right ter link me ter two vicious killers. I look over at Renta. He's gobsmacked.

—Fuck, I sez, —that's it now, then.

—Wot you gonna do? he sez.

—Dunno, I sez.

I sit back, nursin me Pernod. I'm in the shit an there aint no place ter run to.

—Ring up, I sez.

—Who? he sez.

—The police, I sez, —it might as well be you that makes the call. Cos some fucker's gonna do it out of malice. A mate might as well make a butty out of it.

—No way, he sez, —wot do yer take me for? I aint no grass.

—It aint grassin, I sez, —someone's gotta get the twenty grand. An it might as well be you. Take yer kids ter Disneyland.

—No, he sez, an he's adamant.

—But it can't be grassin if yer instructed ter do it by the man yer grassin on, I sez.

He's still shakin his head.

—It aint murder, I sez, —if yer pay someone else ter kill yer.

—Where's this fuckin leadin? he sez, —No fucker OD's in my flat.

—Look, I sez, —I'm gonna walk out of here in twenty minutes an some lousy bastard is gonna grass me up an they're gonna be twenty grand better off. I'd rather it was you.

There's a loud bang on the door.

—Who is it? sez Renta.

—US, shouts a voice. The door goes off its hinges wid the second bang.

There's police everywhere, shoutin an screamin. I'm banged inter the wall an a cut over me eye reopens. Renta's on the floor. A cop's got his head twisted an they're cuffin him.

—Nowt ter do wid him, I sez, —what's the fuckin game?

DS Waine walks in, looks at the empty drink an sez, —plenty of dryin out time now for yer, Drunk.

They cuff me an they lead me an Renta out to the van. They fling us in the back. An Renta for no reason is in the shit nearly as much as me. He's an accessory after the fact an he's also conspired ter pervert the course of justice. An what had he done? Fuck all, just minded his own business.

Karen an Steve leave Mrs Jarvis's bungalow. They're off to see Steve's best mate and soul buddy. They've done Edna proud, Karen thinks. They tidied up and laid her out in her best night dress. Karen watches calmly as Steve double locks the mortice that he and

Thommo fitted on community service. Steve is all a
tizzy, she spots. She'll have to be careful. They head
down Rochdale Road on foot.

—Why the fuck did yer say Mays? asks Karen, —
it's fuckin miles.

—I used ter get me boots there when I was a kid,
Steve says in defence.

—Let's get a bus, she says.

—Fuck off, says Steve, —we might get recognised.
They trudge on.

—What colour van has Charlie got? asks Karen.

—Red Transit, says Steve.

They round past Churnet Street and spot the Transit
in the distance, parked at the bottom of Collyhurst
Street.

—Easy-peasy lemon curd on toast, says Steve.

Karen is less delighted. She's thinking fast. She
needs to get a bit of freedom from Steve so she can
make a phone call on her moby.

They finally reach the van to find Charlie amusing
himself by etching a name on the dashboard.

—What the fuck yer doin? says Steve.

—Firm's van, says Charley.

—Oh right, says Steve, —won't yer get a bollockin?

—I aint stupid enough ter write me own name, he
says, laughin.

Steve grabs Charlie's arm and they hug, with
Charlie leering over Steve's shoulder at Karen as they
do so.

Steve and Karen jump in the Tranny. Steve's in the
front and Karen's in the back, sat on a tool bench. She
can hear every word they say.

—Fit piece, says Charlie.

—She goes like a clockwork Cindy wid new
batteries, says Steve by way of testimonial.

—Wouldn't mind findin out, says Chaz.

191

—Goats I share, says Steve, —women I don't.

—Hey Babs, Steve shouts to Karen, —wanna McDonalds an we can decide what ter do?

—Yeah, says Karen, —an there's no need ter fuckin shout.

So they drive up to the Newton Heath McDonald's, the one on Oldham Road just before the Social. Karen sees that Charlie's staring at her tits through the interior mirror for most of the drive. She guesses he's not had much sex since his release and he's probably paid for what he's had.

—A penny for em, partner? says Steve to Charlie.

—Just thinkin about the good old times, says Charlie.

They get to McDonalds and use the drive-thru to order a Big Mac and Coke each. They park up facing the Oldham Road traffic and have a break. Karen and Steve are finding this robbery and murder lark a bit wearing on the nerves.

—Tell Kaz about the goat, Steve says, trying to lighten the mood.

—You tell her, says Chaz laughin, —it was your idea.

—So yer shagged a goat? asks Karen.

—One of them unanswered questions int it? says Charlie.

—Fuck off, says Steve, —we never did. —We tried, but we got interrupted.

They open their Big Macs, sling the gherkins out the van window and eat what's left.

—Steve, says Kaz, —I need the toilet. Pass us me hat out of me bag, will yer.

A minute later Karen saunters into McDonalds. She heads straight for the Ladies and once there gets her moby out.

She rings a number, hangs up and rings again.

—Hello, says a voice.

—It's me Kaz, she says.

—Where are yer? the voice says.

—No matter, says Karen, —be on the Hartshead services at three o'clock. Got that?

—Yeah but... says the voice.

—No fuckin buts, says Karen, —just fuckin be there.

—Okay, says the voice, —love yer.

—The same an that, says Karen.

She walks out of the toilet. Charlie's there, right outside.

—Right? he says.

She don't like the way he's looking at her tits.

—We gotta be friends Karen, he says, —you need me.

—I do? she says.

—Yeah, he replies, pushing her against the door to the restaurant.

His hands are under her top. She rubs her crotch against his jeans and she can feel the hard on. She rubs it through the material. He pushes her top up.

—Not here, she says, unzipping him, —later. We gotta ditch Steve. She's got her hand on his dick. —Me an you could make it, she says.

—Yeah, he says, tryin to get his hand in her knickers.

—Get me to the Hartshead services for three 'clock, she says, opening her legs a little, —an I'll fuck yer brains out.

Charlie's ready for it now. But just as he's about to drag her into a toilet, the restaurant door bangs into her back. They jump apart thinking it's Steve. But it's only some old punter with his grankids.

—Is there a queue? he says.

—Cheeky fucker, says Karen, and walks out laughing.

She sees Steve watching her walking back. She can tell he's picking up that her tits are lookin perkier then when she went in, and guesses he'll be thinking to keep an eye on his old partner. Which means his full attention will not be on her. Which is exactly how Karen wants it.

I get taken ter Bootle Street Police station an charged in a whirl. Me head's spinnin. Renta's shoutin an screamin about justice. He has ter be bundled away from the charge desk by about four of em.

—Where'd yer get the cuts an abrasions? asks the Desk Sergeant.

—Nothin ter do wid me arrest, I sez.

An it keeps his paperwork easy, so he minds his own business.

They sling me in a cell on me own (I guess I've bin awarded VIP status) I'm left to ponder me life an me new abode. It's no bigger than a snooker table, an it consists of one wrought iron door, one wooden bed an one window about eight feet up. There's no mattress, nowhere ter piss, an no fuckin hope. This is it, a think ter meself, got ter play it right now, or these places are home for the rest of me natural life. An how long will it be before I'm countin the bricks or breadin spiders? I'll probably finish up bein known as the *Spiderman of Strangeways Jail* an end up gettin celebrity buggered by a life boy. I'm dyin for a piss. I notice a bell by the side of the door. There's some writin next ter it that I assume are the instructions about use. I can't wait much longer for the toilet so I wander over ter ring it. I read the message.

Want sex?
then ring this bell and a cunt will come.

I ring the bell about twenty times an no cunt comes. Then a realise it's turned off or disconnected, or maybe just bein ignored. Some sorta mind game maybe. Or maybe not, cos yer can't think straight when yer mind's constantly on not pissin yer pants. An I know I aint gonna be havin no bad dreams ternight, cos I aint gonna be able ter sleep. I'm left ter ponder me future. Then a strange thing happens. I hear a voice singin. It's some kid that's got busted. The tune's AfroMan's *Cos I Got High* though he was putting his own words to it,

'I got kicked out a school
Cos a got high'.

He went on for about ten minutes rippin everythin an everybody ter pieces usin the AfroMan tune. The kid's got style. I make me own version up an sing it back at him,

'I lost me home an wife
Cos a got drunk...'

Me an the kid have a conversation through the wall.

—What yer bin nicked for? he shouts.

—Murder an that, I shout, —what about you?

—Writin poetry, he sez. —Who yer kill? Yer wife?

—No one, I sez, —I aint killed no one or done nothin.

—Wanna hear the poem that I wrote on the bus shelter? he shouts, an it's obvious he's still high.

—SHUT THE FUCK UP, shouts Renta, —let's get some fuckin kip!

We go quiet. I stand in the middle of the bare floor, survey me options a bit before lyin flat on me back an starin at the ceilin light. There's complete silence. I start ter think how all this will effect me kids an me mam. It don't bear thinkin about. I try to clear me head an think of some path through this mess. God, I need a piss.

I hear what I think is rain on the little skylight

window an a mull over the idea of standin on me bed ter try an look out. But I'd have ter drag me bed across to the other side of the cell an somehow I don't think movin furniture is in the terms of me lease. I look at me wrist where me watch woulda bin if they hadn't had taken it, an I wonder wot fuckin time it is. More sensory deprivation, I think ter meself. I try ter relocate the bed, only ter find it's fixed where it is.

I hear a door clangin down the corridor. The noise sends a shiver down me spine. It's as if someone's walked over my grave, an I've an idea there could be a million more clangs from where that one came from. About ten minutes later an me cell door opens an a young copper I aint seen before comes in.

—Piss? he sez.

An I've never felt so relieved in me life.

We walk down the corridor; an he opens a door wid one pan in it.

—Hurry up, he sez an stands watchin.

I finish an don't get chance ter wash me hands. He leads me back ter me cell widout sayin another word.

About half an hour later me cell door opens an it's DS Waine.

—Right, he sez, —tea for yer. How's the nerves?

—Wot? I sez.

—A bit early yet, he adds, —but soon yer'll be crawlin the walls for a pint or a snort.

—Bin there before, I sez, —the first ten days is the hardest.

—Yeah, he sez, takin the piss, —the ten year after that'll be a piece a cake.

—No thanks, I sez takin the piss back, —I had a biscuit before I came out.

Waine smiles an sez, —here's one for yer. Who is the most famous man buried in Moston Cemetery?

—The man who invented the crossword puzzle, I

sez, spoilin his joke.

—Thanks, he sez smilin.

An I know it was no joke. I'd just bin Joe Columbo'd. Mr Smartarse always has ter know everythin, now I've given him somethin ter work on.

DC Waine walks as if ter leave. As he's goin he turns an sez, —Who's the Chinaman?

—Billy Kelly, I sez.

—Why? he sez.

So I explain. At the end of it, he falls about laffin.

—We're gearin up for a Triad war an it's some Miles Plattin drunk, he sez, —gotta tell this one ter George.

I smile back an he stops laffin. —That means you're the brains then, he sez, an shuts me door with a bang.

I hear Waine walkin along the corridor whistlin. I aint much good at body language an that, but I don't feel in me water that it's a good sign for me.

Me door has bin shut about as long as it took for the cllllllllllaaaaaaaannng ter leave me head when it's opened again.

First for breakfast, which is a mug of tea an scrambled egg on somethin that had enjoyed a brief an unsuccessful relationship wid the toaster. I'm not hungry an me nerves are shaky but I manage ter get the tea down me. Just as I finish the tea, the door opens again.

—Interview time, sez a fresh faced DS Coyle.

I'm led ter the interview room, where I'm explained all about the tape, an me rights, an I decline a solicitor. Shuttleworth starts in on me.

—For the benefit of the tape we are now showin the accused some pictures of William Patrick Kelly, also known as the Chinaman.

—Just back from the chemists, sez Coyle, an passes

me a handful of pictures.

I look at the first one. Me stomach turns. It's of a contorted Billy. I might be wrong but I don't think the end came as a merciful release. His face is screwed up, his eyes are bulgin an the only thing I can think of that describes what he looked like is this fish I ate in Benidorm. I can't remember its name but they served it wid the head still on an the eyes starin yer down. An no way did that fish or Billy die happy, they died fuckin traumatised. I gotta save me sanity so I change me thoughts. I'm in a police cell, holdin a picture of Billy lyin dead on the floor, but in me mind I'm on a Benidorm beach I once holidayed at, takin the piss out of a Scouser who can't swim. I start laffin at the memory. I try ter stop meself but I can't.

DS Coyle looks at DC Shuttleworth an sez, —For the benefit of the tape the accused is laffin at a picture of William Patrick Kelly lyin dead on his lounge floor.

—This interview terminated at eleven twenty-three, sez Shuttleworth.

—Me an Terry here are off for a pint now, sez Coyle, a little shook up.

—It'll be a long time before you have a pint again, sez Shuttleworth.

—Let me tell yer something, he sez, —tonight, while me an Terry here are havin a pint an a game of snooker, you'll be in your cell, pacin up an down. Makin up one story an then changin it, then changin it back again. An then thinkin up an entirely different story. Then you'll start thinkin about getting a solicitor, then start thinkin you won't need one, cos you're gonna do a deal. Then you'll start pacin up an down again. An all that thinkin an all that pacin will have took you roughly four minutes.

It's a tried an trusted method of unsettlin a suspect, a method passed down from policeman ter policeman.

198

An it works. I'm shittin meself.

—What do you prefer colons or semicolons? asks Shuttleworth.

What? I sez, confused.

—Because that's the level of your input into your confession tomorrow. You get to choose the grammar.

They leave, laffin heartily as they go. The door slams shut. An if they'd of left me wid me shoelaces, I'd be doin a Fred West.

THE EDGE

Karen an Steve are heading east on the M62. They've gone past Birch Services and are about ten minutes away from Hartshead Services. The mood of the party is subdued. They've just heard on the news about the Drunk and Carl's arrest and about another local somebody called Vinny Doherty's murder.

—Fuck me, says Karen, —Drunk's got all sorts on the payroll.

—We get ter Spain, says Steve, —an when we get settled there, we give it a bit of time an we come back an we get the Drunk out.

Karen thinks it sounds good but, even as he's saying it, Steve knows it isn't going to happen.

—What we need is a plan, says Charlie.

—Fuck off, says Steve, —that's how it all began in the first place.

They cruise along at sixty an hour. Karen listens in on the chatter between Charlie and Steve.

—Refuel at Hartshead Services, says Charlie.

—Yer've got three quarters of a tank left, says Steve.

—I'm gonna need a full tank, says Charlie, —in case of detours or road blocks or a bit of a run-around in Hull. I got a good contact there, sound lad, called, 'Is that you Arry'.

—Funny fuckin name, says Steve.

—Not really, says Chaz, —he's got a hunchback an his name is Harry.

—Oh, says Steve.

—What's bein a hunchback got ter do wid anythin? says Karen.

—It's ter do with bein in the nick, says Charlie.

—Oh, says Karen, losin interest. She studies her watch. She's about four minutes away from freedom. If Steve wants a boiled egg she's just about got enough time left to do one for him. Anything more than that and he'll have to see Charlie.

—We've met before, DS Waine sez.

—At the casino, I sez.

—No, he sez, —it took me a while ter figure the where an when.

This fucker does think he's Joe Columbo.

—I was waitin for me breakfast this mornin, he sez, —an it came ter me. Outside a school in Newton Heath, that's where I saw you.

—Wot you sayin? I ask.

—About six months ago. We got a phone call about a suspicious character hangin round a school. So we investigate an it was some poor fucker that's goin through a divorce who's tryin ter see his kid. That poor fucker was you.

An I remember it. I'd stopped seein me kids. Nothin ter do wid the ex-wife. It was my decision. In a drunken temper I'd decided that I could no longer be a 'Saturday Dad'. An regardless ter any hurt it may of caused me kids, I kept it up. I dint write, visit or phone. It hurt bad but the vodka eased the ache an the weed helped the pain. An I'd decided never ter physically touch or be physically touched by another human bein again as long as I lived. If I ordered a pint, I'd put the money on the counter an say, —Keep the change. If anybody accidentally touched me I'd wince. Me head was gone too. I was talkin ter meself an the furniture. This one day it got ter me bad, I've just got ter see me little girl, Shannon. So I go down to the school an I hang round by the bus stop outside. I've forgot me watch an I realise I've missed playtime so I've got ter wait till dinner time for the next time she comes inter the yard. I go in the pub opposite bang on eleven an down three pints in about twenty minutes. I aint ate or slept, I've had vodka for breakfast, so I'm rockin on me feet. I walk back over. I'm askin strangers the time an starin in the playground. It's about five minutes before they come out when I get a tap on me shoulder. I turn an it's a young copper.

—Wot's your game? he sez.

A concerned neighbour had noticed me erratic behaviour an rang the police.

I'm pissed up an pissed off.

—Dominoes, I sez, an turn back towards the school yard.

He grabs me an pushes me against the wire.

—Leave it, sez a voice, —put him in the car.

An that voice apparently was DS Waine.

They march me over to the car, duck me head, an shut the door. They get in the front, not as in act of trust yer understand, but because the car doors are automatically locked an I couldn't do a runner if I wanted to.

—Wot's yer problem? sez Waine.

—Look if yer arrestin me, I sez, —just fuckin arrest me.

—Good idea, sez PC Dunphy, —an I'll slap yer fuckin face if yer swear again.

—Listen mate, sez Waine, —I don't wanna arrest no one. I don't like paperwork. So tell me wot yer doin outside a school in a drunken state?

—That's my business, I sez.

—What sort of man cries? sez Dunphy.

I put me hand ter me face. I'm cryin. That was the first time I ever cried widout knowin it. Afterwards I couldn't seem ter stop.

Then there's a bang on the window. It's Shannon. She'd watched it all from her classroom window. She was just turned seven then.

—Dad! she sez.

A teacher comes out an they lead Shannon back in. All her classmates are against the wire fence watchin an shoutin an laffin. Shannon's cryin. Waine gets out of the car an has a word wid a teacher. The teacher knows me. Waine gets back in the car.

—Why dint yer tell us? he sez.

—Tell yer what? I sez.

—We're human beins as well yer know, he sez, — I've bin divorced an done things as daft as this. I'm takin yer home an yer stayin home. If yer go anywhere near that fuckin school again I'll kick yer fuckin arse. Understand?

—Yeah, I sez, an I never went back.

—Remember the school? sez Waine.

—I do, I sez, —yer did me a favour there.

—Right, he sez, —start ter finish. I wanna know wot went on. An I wanna know where Tucker an Reilly are now.

So I start ter give him the truth, only it's a truth that few see apart from me. I tell him how the plan ter rob the casino was just a plot for a book that got out of hand. Told him I hadn't had anythin ter do wid any of the murders an no hand in the robbery. An that I dint know where Steve an Karen were. An I dint really, I know they said they were goin ter Hull, but that was yesterday. Anythin coulda happened since then.

DS Waine lost patience an terminated the interview.

Karen, Steve and Charlie are just pulling into Hartshead Services.

—She's one of them obsessives, says Charlie describing his neurotic wife, —even puts her fridge magnets in alphabetical order. Alicante before

203

Weymouth an that.

—Why? says Steve.

Karen's listening to them, but she's looking round the Services.

—Dunno, says Charlie, —an get this one. Before she throws out the old papers she puts em in date order, mornin papers on the bottom, evenin papers on the top. Magazines go last in alphabetical order. If somethin's out monthly, that's behind them. I tell yer, it can take half the fuckin night.

—Has she had treatment? asks Kaz.

—Treatment? says Charlie, —she's baffled a dozen doctors. She stacks food in brand name order. When she takes down the Christmas cards it's gotta be done in date received order.

—Fascinatin, says Karen, as Charlie pulls up and parks in a discreet place out of sight.

Karen likes what she's seeing.

They sit there a second.

Anybody want anythin? says Chaz.

—Get us couple a magazines, says Kaz, buying a bit of time, —an bring em back in alphabetic order.

Charlie smiles.

—You want anythin? Charlie says to Steve.

—No, says Steve.

—Go wid him Babs, says Karen.

—Naw, says Steve, —too many people seen me picture.

—Put yer hat on, says Chaz.

—No, says Steve, and slouches back.

Karen becomes agitated. She looks at the gun in Steve's belt as she's watching Charlie fuel up with the other eye.

She looks over at Steve. He looks asleep. She lifts her top up for Charlie to see. He's as bitten as the rest, she thinks.

Charlie goes to pay for the fuel.

—Steve, wake up, Karen says, elbowing him in the ribs.

—What? he says.

—Follow Charlie, she says, —get him in the toilet. He's got a mobile.

—So? says Steve.

—When we were in McDonald's I thought I seen him ringin someone.

—Who? says Steve, having trouble comprehending.

—I don't know, says Karen, —'Is that you 'Arry' maybe. He was dead keen we had ter stop here.

—Too fuckin true, says Steve, jumping up and grabbing a spanner, —an he had three quarters of a tank. Wait here, Babs, I'll see what's goin on.

Steve trots off after Charlie. Karen watches his chubby bum wobble its way into the service station. She scrawls Steve a hurried note and jumps out of the van carrying the bag of money. Over the other side of the car park a Volkswagen Polo beeps its horn.

DC Coyle together wid DC Hussain are interviewin me again.

—So you accept no guilt for the robbery of the casino? sez Coyle.

—None, I sez.

—Yer know where yer'll finish, don't yer? sez Coyle.

—I'm innocent, I sez.

—Bollocks, sez Hussain, —conspiracy definite. An the rest provable just as soon as we arrest yer buddies.

—You're gonna go ter Rampton, sez Coyle, —an yer never comin out. Cos you'll be sectioned under the Mental Health Act.

The blood drains from me face. Coyle's tail's up. He can smell fear.

—Interview terminated at fifteen twenty three, he sez.

—I'd think about that solicitor now, sez Hussain.

Steve follows Charlie into the toilets and looks around. There's no one about. He waits while Charlie takes his dick out. He gets his nerves settled. He's just about to banjo his mate when he gets a coughing fit.

—Yer wanna watch that cough, says Charlie, looking round.

—Bit a tonsillitis, says Steve.

—Monsalitus more like, says Charlie, —it's wot yer get for goin down on Karen.

—What? says Steve.

—She's a one that Karen, says Charlie, —showed me her tits while you was asleep. Told me ter get you here for three. An she.....................

Steve finally puts it together. He turns and runs back towards the car.

Karen climbs into the front passenger seat of the Voltswagen Polo of window cleaner, Denis Moss, ex partner of the deceased Maurice Fallon. Steve was partly right. When he'd seen her climb into the firm's van, he'd immediately thought it was the prettier of the two window cleaners she was taking off with. But looks wasn't everything, Karen reflects, and if Steve had sought a second opinion then a mirror would have told him that looks isn't high on her list of boyfriend must-haves. Karen puts Steve out of her mind. —Right Babs, says Karen, —Agadir here we come.

Denis Moore smiles and puts it in first. Just as they drive away, they see Steve running to the Transit van.

Trailing behind trying to do up his buttons is Charlie Marley.

—Put yer foot down, Denis, Karen says.

Steve gets to the van. Karen's left him the keys on top of a note, but no money.

He reads the note and he takes the spanner out of his back pocket. He passes the note to Charlie. Charlie reads it to himself, lips moving as he does so.

Dear Steve,
Sorry an that.
It was good an that
Off abroad.
Charlie stuck his dick in me mouth
in McDonald's.
He wants ter fuck you
>   *Love*
>   *Karen*
>   *X*
P.S. Good luck.

—No mate, says Charlie and drops the note. Just as Steve slams a spanner into his temple. Charlie staggers backwards. Steve swipes him again. Charlie hits the deck and he's face down. Steve gives him one good last whack on the back of the neck. He can hear voices. He bundles Charlie into the van. He looks round. Everything's all right apart from a bit of blood. He picks the note up and stuffs it in Charlie's mouth.

—Goats I share, he says, —women I don't.

There's a huffling an a puffling from Charlie. Steve looks down. Charlie's blowing blood bubbles.

—Shut the fuck up, shouts Steve and slings the music on. It's some rock-a-day Johnny singin, 'Tell

207

yer mar...tell yer par...our love's gonna grow...wah wah'.

Steve heads for the only place he knows. Miles Plattin.

DS Waine comes in ter tell me some news.

—We've got a Magistrates Order ter detain yer for a further forty eight hours, he sez.

—Then I can go home? I ask. Me nerves are shakin.

—Don't be daft, DS Waine sez, —you aint goin home this decade.

I aint done nothin, I sez.

An then he tells me the flaw in my version.

—Yer know wot stops your version workin? he sez.

I'm all ears. I bin goin through this thing in me mind over an over, an I need constructive criticism before I get ter meet the jury.

—The key is the key, he sez.

—The key? I ask, —what key?

—The key ter Bella's door, he sez.

I go white. An I realise that I'm snookered an the only reason he's tellin this ter me is ter demoralise me. Which he just fuckin has.

—That's the little thread that unravels the jumper of this case, he sez. —Don't be a mug, Drunk, he continues, —tell us what yer know.

He shuts the door an goes whistlin away. Me head is spinnin.

The key? I think, *why the fuck dint I think a that?*

Steve is heading back along the M62, only this time he's going West. He looks calm. He's singing some Cliff Richard song about travelling light.

—Not as light as yer think, says Charlie, spitting Karen's letter out of his mouth.

Steve swerves the car in fear. He backhands Charlie, pulls out the gun and says, —One move, Charlie an yer dead.

But Charlie can't move. The slap has knocked him backward and impaled him on the screwdriver that he'd been carving with in the mornin. Charlie wheezes and cries a bit. Which Steve just about hears over the sounds of the traffic. Steve takes a wrong turn. Which means somewhere going through his native Salford, Charlie dies. He makes as if to get up, says, —Mam, then falls back dead.

Steve drives along Oldham Road, oblivious to the world. He hasn't a clue where he's going. He's lost without Karen or the Drunk, and now he's lost his best mate as well. He's tired. He turns at Varley Street and heads down it. As he passes Sawley Road he notices he's being followed. He puts this down as paranoia and parks up outside Corpus Christie. The car behind parks up. He clocks the number plate. It's an unmarked car. He tucks the gun into the top of his jeans and unbuckles his seat belt. He can't make his mind up whether to take a hostage or run.

He runs to the car pointing the gun alternately at DC Shuttleworth and DC Hussain.

—Get out, Steve says, —lie on the floor. Give me your fuckin cuffs.

Hussain passes him his cuffs.

—An a key, says Steve, —hurry fuckin up.

Hussain passes him the key.

They're both lying on the pavement. People are walkin by, but Steve's waving a gun so they steer clear. He gets Hussain's hands and he's just about to handcuff them behind his back when he hears a siren. So he's no alternative but to take it on his toes. In one hand he's got a gun, in the other hand he's got the handcuffs.

He breaks into a sprint, ducks in behind Corpus, and starts gaspin for breath as he runs through the Walks and Closes. The world's swimming round him. He comes out on Sawley Road and starts runnin across the Green there. From two different directions, police vans converge. He turns back and heads for Albert Court, the former home of Billy Kelly. As he gets there, the caretaker is talking to some old guy and his granddaughter who's aged about nine. Steve tear-arses right up and puts the gun to the head of the caretaker.

—Got a key ter the roof? he says.

—Yeah, he says.

—Give, says Steve.

The caretaker gives Steve the key.

—OPEN THIS, he yells pointin to the Tower Block door.

The Caretaker opens it.

—Stay back! Steve shouts to the police.

The police form a line about twenty yard away, there's maybe eight of them.

Steve grabs the little girl and puts the gun to her head.

He walks through the Tower Block door, using the little girl as a shield.

The grandad is frantic. —Please don't hurt her, he's saying.

—I won't hurt a kid, says Steve, —what yer take me for?

He presses for both lifts. The first one arrives and he keeps it on hold till the second one gets down. He sends the first lift up but presses every button. Then he waves his gun at the Police circling outside and jumps in the second lift. He presses Twelve and it heads on up. He gets to the top, and opens the door to the roof ladder. He locks it behind, and him and the little girl are on the roof. He takes her to the side and sits her on the low wall. She daren't look down. She's shaking and crying.

—It's all right, says Steve, —I aint never hit no kid. Yer safe wid me.

The handcuffs are miles too small for her hands. So he throws them over the wall and off the roof. He gets a piece of rope that's holding some wood together and ties one end round him and one end round the little girl. They're both sat on the edge of the wall round the roof. If Steve falls, jumps or gets shot, then the kid goes with him. In his hand he's holding the gun.

—What's yer name? Steve says to the little girl.

—Lyndsey Collier, she says.

—Is yer dad Tom Collier? says Steve.

Lyndsey's cryin. —Yeah, she says.

—Small world, says Steve, —I used ter play darts wid him. Tell him I was askin when yer see him.

Steve takes a peek. Down below a crowd's gathering. And the police are there in force.

—Who's Charlie Marley an what part does he have in all this? DS Coyle is askin me.

—Some mate of Tuckers, I sez, —I've never met him.

—Come on, he sez, —you wrote it, dint yer? What part did yer write for Charlie?

—It aint like that, I sez, —I just had this simple plot for a book. It's Tucker an Reilly that took the idea an used it. I did nothin.

—We've just found Marley's dead body in a Transit,

Coyle sez ter shock me.

But frankly after the week I've had, it ud take a bit more than that ter make me raise an eyebrow.

—How can I be responsible for the death of someone I aint even met?

—I think you cohersed Tucker an Riley, he sez, —I think you plotted an planned everythin. An that you had a little network. You supplied them with the where an the when. You got the gun off a Chinese contact. You gave them the key ter Bella's house. An you decided who they killed. You my son are as guilty as sin. An we've got all the evidence we need. So let's start again. Who's Charley Marley an what part does he have in all this?

I sit back. I can see which way their case against me is gonna go. I am ter be marked down as the ring leader. An they're gonna try an implicate me in the murders. So much for helpin em. They can fuck off from here on in.

Steve has gone to great pains to explain to the police below that if he goes Lyndsey goes as well. He's also gone to greater pains to explain to Lyndsey that he has no intentions of harming her. Lyndsey is hysterical because she can't tell which Steve is telling the truth. The one waving the gun and tugging the rope who's shouting about death. Or the nice calm one who's saying, 'No one's gonna hurt yer, it'll be all right when the Drunk gets here'.

A police negotiator starts on a megaphone:

—Steve, he says, —wot yer gotta do is remain calm. Nobody is threatenin you. There are people down here who would like ter help yer.

—SHOOT THE BASTARD, shouts an interested bystander.

—Arrest that little cunt, the negotiator shouts, pointing at the interested bystander. This makes Steve smile.

The negotiator continues:

—In every story, Steve, there's your side an there's their side an somewhere in the middle is the truth. An Steve all we're interested in is everybody comin down safe. What I want you to do Steve is move from the edge an let me come up an talk. Can I come up there, Steve?

—You'll go back down faster if yer fuckin try, shouts Steve.

—Wot do you want, Steve? he says.

—Right firstly, shouts Steve, —give that fuckin megaphone ter someone who aint a refugee from the Jerry Springer show.

—Haha, says the man and tries to continue.

—Don't laugh at me yer tosser, Steve shouts, —give the megaphone ter someone else.

Steve watches. Someone else takes the megaphone just as the press an cameras arrive.

—Right Tucker, the new man sez, through the megaphone, —I want the child down unharmed. What do you want from me? No nonsense, he carries on. —No planes ter Rio de Janeiro. No million pound in a suitcase. What do you want?

Steve thinks hard.

—Who are you? he says, wantin ter make sure he wasn't talkin to the local lollipop man.

Back comes the voice:

—I'm Detective Inspector George Mulcahy an today I will arrest you.

—Right George, says Steve laughing, —in the meantime I want a litre bottle of vodka, a litre bottle of coke an twenty Dorchester. Can yer manage that?

—Not a chance son, says George, breaking every

213

rule in the book for dealing with these sort of cases.

—What? shouts Steve tugging at the rope and making Lyndsey move about like a string driven puppet.

—'I got no strings ter hold me down', sings Steve.

Lyndsey is sobbing.

—Well? Steve shouts.

—I'm not lettin you get tanked up while that little girl's life depends on your sanity. I have a daughter meself. Release her an you have George Mulcahy's word that you'll get that vodka.

—No, shouts Steve, —we'll do a deal.

—What's yer proposal? says Mulcahy, and something in his voice tells Steve he's quite enjoying this.

—You send up the vodka, the coke an the cigs, says Steve, —delivered by the Drunk. An when he gets here, before any drink is drunk, I'll release Lyndsey. An one way or another, after we've had our drink, we'll come down. You have Steven Tucker's word on that.

—Done, shouts a jubilant George Mulcahy, and puts the megaphone down.

—You've got one hour, shouts Steve, —or me an Lyndsey 'Believe we can fly'.

I look at DC Waine an then I look at DC Shuttleworth. I'm stunned.

—No fuckin chance, I sez.

—Wot? sez Waine, disbelievin.

—If I go up there he'll kill me, I sez, —like he's killed every other fucker.

—If yer don't the sick bastard'll end up tippin that poor kid off the block, sez Shuttleworth.

—Why would he kill the kid? I sez, —the kid's done him no harm.

—Why? screams Waine, —he killed the dog an a pensioner dint he? Get fuckin real.

—If he'll kill them then he'll kill me, I sez in defence.

—Yer cowardly little shit, sez Waine, —it's the life of a nine year old kid an it's in your hands.

An somethin in what he sez touches me. I think about the nine year old African kid dyin for the want of six fuckin quid. An I think a Billy Kelly an how it hurt him. I think of poor Sheila Grimes in that fridge. An I think about me own little girl. An I remember DC Waine not arrestin me at the school that day. An I find meself sayin, —I'll do it, but I want it mentionin in court if I live. I get some sorta commendation, right?

—Of course, sez Waine, an I can tell he's lyin.

—Goes without sayin, nods Shuttleworth.

They quickly go through some procedure ter release me. An then we're headin back towards Miles Plattin, with me in the back of the zoomin police car thinkin, *This is it, kidder.* We're travellin down Oldham road inter the Miles Plattin of me youth. A first came ter this place when it was all brand new. They'd pulled down the slums and built a new Miles Plattin, made up of flat roofed maisonettes an tower blocks. We were just kids, brand new in the world as well, an it was a paradise playground of canals an railway yards, of long summers an darin deeds. I lived here wid me mam an me dad an me two brothers in an upstairs maisonette next to a rubbish chute. In summer we were haunted by flies, an in winter the under floor heatin wouldn't work. At night the Walks an Closes rang wid the drunken voices of people wanderin home from the pubs. They'd be yellin an laffin an arguin an singin. An me an me little brother would be perched on our bedroom winda sill, half asleep but still jokin, an we'd watch the Saturday night maritals erupt, men an women screamin an swearin an doors slammin. Long into the night yer could hear the roars, yer'd fall asleep listenin.

Yer knew everyone an everyone knew you an yer felt a part of somethin, yer felt wanted. An somewhere along the line I changed, an so did Miles Plattin.

We get ter Albert Court wid about ten minutes of the hour left. I refuse ter get out of the car until they take the handcuffs off.

—No can do, sez DI Mulcahy.

—Right, I sez, —drive me back then.

Mulcahy can see that I got him. He takes off the cuffs an I get out a the car.

—If yer try ter run, sez DC Shuttleworth, —I'll break both yer fuckin legs.

—Run ter where? I sez.

Steve's watchin it all from above.

—Is that you, Drunk? he shouts.

—Yeah, I sez.

—You got the drink? he sez.

—Wot fuckin drink? I sez.

An he tells me that he's bin promised a bottle of vodka an a bottle a coke.

—Who the fuck's payin for this? shouts some nosy fucker, —The fuckin tax payer?

—Fuck off, I sez ter the interferin twat.

—Who you tellin ter fuck off? shouts Steve.

—Some mouthy fucker down here, I shout.

The Police push the line of civilians back ten yards.

—Drunk, shouts Steve, —go ter the Asians on the corner an get it. An you pick the bottles. I don't trust these fuckers not ter inject the bottle wid knock-out drops or somethin.

An can I fuck believe what I'm hearin. A murderer is sendin an arrested man ter the off licence an the police are gonna be payin.

I accompany two PC'S ter the offy an I get what was requested plus four Stellas, two bars of fruit an nut an two plastic cups. I aint had a can for days so I down me first one in the offy.

The shopkeeper wants payin.

—Sorry, I sez pattin me pockets, —skint.

DC Shuttleworth an DC James club tergether ter pay for the drink.

We head back ter the tower block. It's a media circus. George Mulcahy has gone out on a limb on this one. He has staked his professional career on me bein exchanged for that little girl. If that girl don't live now, he's on the dole come Monday. Rather that or compulsory retired wid a nervous breakdown an a huge pension.

I'm ready ter go up. Mulcahy sez ter me,

—Don't try nothin heroic.

I look at him like he wants ter be locked up not be doin the lockin up. —Listen, I sez, —you keep your marksmen trained on him at all times. An the first available opportunity after the kid's safe an I'm not in the picture, yer shoot him. Understand?

I cross ter the Tower Block doors, accompanied by a uniformed constable. I go in an head for the lift. There's two plain clothes officers waitin. They go up wid me. But they wait in the lift. I'm met by a little man wid a limp. Apparently he's the trained negotiator.

—Whatever yer do, he sez, —don't rush him.

—I'll fight the urge, I sez.

At the top it's bedlam. There's four armed officers with their sights trained on the door. I'm about ter go through, an two CID are in me way, arguin with each other.

—You bin on the course, sez DC Froggatt, —get out there an try an talk him down.

—Fuck off, sez James, —you've got a

commendation for that pregnant woman on the maisonettes. You go.

—She was two floors up not fuckin twelve, sez Frog, —an anyway I was cuffed ter the veranda an she wasn't pointin no gun at me snotter.

Either side of em are two armed officers, crouched an ready for action.

—Who's in charge? I ask.

—I am, sez a bulky officer.

—I aint goin in that door while you lot are pointin guns at it, I sez.

—Calm down, sez the Negotiator.

—Fuck off, I sez, —I aint goin through that door wid this lot trainin guns on it.

—These men are trained ter handle these sorts a situation, he sez.

—Yeah an they got body armour an I aint, I sez, —they either go down a floor or I go down twelve.

There's a stand off.

The negotiator sends em down a floor. Froggatt an James back away.

I knock an sez, —Open up, Steve.

Steve opens the door. He's usin the girl as a shield.

—'Welcome to my world', he sings.

The negotiator tries his luck wid Steve.

—Steve, the negotiator sez, —now might be a good time ter talk.

—Too late ter talk, sez Steve, —get in, Drunk.

I slide in past Steve an the girl. Steve slips the rope from around the girl an gently pushes her out, slammin an boltin the door after her. We're alone on the roof, just me an him.

—What do yer want? I ask.

—Last drink, he sez.

An I smile.

—The police do that ter yer face? he sez.

—Naw, I sez, —some kid outside an offy.

He laughs.

—Did it though, dint we, Drunk? he sez.

We're stood on the far side of the roof. I've got the bag of drink in me hand. He's holdin the gun. I take the vodka out.

—What happened ter Karen? I ask.

—Dunno, he sez, —she done a runner.

—Who wid? I ask.

—Not got a fuckin clue, he sez.

Steve wanders over to the edge carryin a vodka. I'm stood directly behind him. A thought occurs ter me, miss him by an inch an I'm dead. I move ter the side an look over the top. I immediately go dizzy.

—Twenty snipers aimin at yer as we speak, I sez.

—Gotta go sometime, he sez.

—Yeah, I agree.

I sit down an refill our plastic cups.

We look down an we can see em puttin the little girl in an ambulance.

—You've got fifteen minutes ter come down, shouts George on the megaphone. You can hear in his voice he's ready ter close the curtains on the corpse of the case.

Steve looks over the edge.

—Fancy it, Drunk? he sez.

—What? I sez, knowin exactly what he means.

—Just like Butch Cassidy an the Sundance Kid, he sez, —tie ourselves ter the rope an jump. One small step for a man an all that.

I move away from the edge. —Not for me Steve, I sez, —I'm innocent. I've done fuck all.

Steve laffs his balls off an swigs on his vodka.

—Did yer ever fuck Karen? he asks.

—Never, I lie.

—Cheers for that, Drunk, he sez.

An I can see the madness in his eyes.

—Do yer believe in God? he sez.

I can hear em gettin ready on the stairs. I decide ter keep his mind occupied. The last thing I need is him firin a shot off an the *Shoot Out At The OK Coral* bein re-enacted.

—Vanity not believin in him, I sez, —cos if there aint no God then we're it, aint we? Mankind's top of the tree. An that's a shit scenario.

He aint listenin. His eyes are glazed over, he's buildin his courage up.

—Yer know who I can't understand? he sez.

For some reason I think he's gonna say Karen.

—The thief that wouldn't repent, he sez, —I mean, why din't he? He had nothin ter lose. He might as well have slung in wid Jesus.

—No, I sez, —the thief that didn't repent had it right. We've made our beds, just gotta lie in em.

We agree ter disagree.

We're stood, plastic cups in hand, starin out at the Miles Plattin we grew up in.

—Yer know what makes Miles Plattin special? I ask, pourin meself what could be me last vodka for a very long time.

What? he sez, hoverin over the edge.

—The sense of humour, I sez, —I like ter think that if there'd a bin a lad from Miles Plattin or Monsall in that Black Hole a Calcutta then just before the Nawab of Bengal woulda shut the door, the Plattin lad woulda shouted, 'Yer'd a got another seven in if yer'd a put us in sideways'. An they'd a all still suffocated, but they'd a suffocated laffin. An the Nawab would a had his day spoilt.

—Yeah, but yer can't beat authority, sez Steve, —an I should know. I had that kicked inter me when I was thirteen.

He breaks off a piece a chocolate.

—'Nuts whole hazelnuts', he sings, but it's in a preoccupied voice.

He eats the piece.

—Yer can finish the drink, he sez, —I've had enough.

He stands on the edge, half his feet on the parapet an the other half in the air. He's lookin at me an not at where he's about ter go. He raises the gun an points it at me.

The clock of me life is on halt.

DI George Mulcahy picks up the megaphone.

—Sit down Tucker, he yells, —don't be a bloody fool. We have a plan for a resolution to this.

As he's sayin this, he's signallin for the stormin of the roof.

There's a crashin like a batterin ram. The door splinters. Three armed officers bounce onter the roof. Tear gas explodes.

—Freeze, one shouts.

I freeze like a coke sniffer's left nostril in a snow storm.

There's three guns trained on Steve.

—Should a jump Drunk? he shouts ter me.

—Yer gotta, I shout, —fuck all left for yer here.

Steve nods, teeters on the brink.

—'Wish me luck as you wave me goodbye', he sings.

Then he blows a hole in the side of his head the size of a beer mat. He tilts backwards inter space an falls ter earth.

Everybody is bawlin an shoutin an screamin an pushin. I'm grabbed, slung against the wall an frog-marched down the stairs. I'm cuffed again, an they drag me out a the tower block.

Cameras pan an flashlights click, an someone shouts, 'It's the Drunk, they got the Drunk!' A crowd a kids watch me get put in the van.

An the one thing that they can't take away from me is that me plan actually worked. Cos not one penny of the £194,473 ever got caught. Course, I'm pleadin not guilty, it was just the plot of a book, that's my line, an I'm stickin to it. An when it's all over, me an the kids are gonna go ice-skatin in Central Park an we're gonna laff an laff tergether, like we used ter.

PRAISE FOR MIKE DUFF'S FIRST NOVEL, *LOW LIFE*

"Rooftop Rafferty is no lovable rogue: he's into cheque-book fraud and would probably have your wallet and cards in the time it takes to read the back cover of this book. But despite a career as a one-man Manchester crime wave, and his belief that every good sentence should be cemented in place with an obscenity, he is an engaging character who nods knowingly towards Dickens." - *The Guardian*

"Duff paints a picture of a life most of us couldn't even begin to imagine, let alone survive but he does it with humanity, humour and tremendous insight. What's more, he could teach a few vastly more experienced writers a thing or two about pace, narrative and dialogue." - *The Big Issue*

"It's very fast and very funny, richocheting between caustic social comment and moments of real tenderness." - *City Life*

"In an expertly-structured, witty, pacy book, the author pulls off the remarkable feat of making a central character who's relentlessly nasty in what he does, postively sympathetic." - *News North West*

"Imagine Dostoevsky writing for Viz and you've got some idea of the sharp ugly comedy to be found here." - *Manchester Metro*